C0-API-087

The Music Man from Norway

By Doris Stensland

The Music Man from Norway
Copyright © 2006 by
Doris Stensland

All Rights Reserved

This work may not be used in any form,
or reproduced by any means,
in whole or in part,
without written permission
from the publisher.

ISBN: 0-9759456-4-5

Library of Congress Control Number: 2006933818

Stensland Books
3121 South 102 Street
Omaha Nebraska 68124
www.stenslandbooks.com

Printed in the United States of America

PINE HILL PRESS
4000 West 57th Street
Sioux Falls, SD 57106

Dedication

To my daughter Susan,
who is always there for me,
and who made this book possible.

Preface

This fictional work is grounded in historical facts that I have gathered on the life of Professor Andrew Indseth, a musician from Norway who brought music to southeastern South Dakota at the turn of the century.

I first heard of Professor Indseth from my mother many years ago. As a young girl she knew about him and his music because her uncles, Martin and Tony Overseth, were members of his bands. When examining old newspapers in the Canton Public Library, I came across Professor Indseth's name very often. In 1987, I received a letter from the wife of one of Professor Indseth's grandsons, ordering some of my former books. This lady included a packet with copies of newspaper clippings about Professor Indseth and a family record of his life. All of this information increased my interest in his life.

In the 1890's and the turn of the century, there was neither radio, television, nor movies, and the Professor helped fill the need for entertainment in those days. This was an interesting time of Chautauquas and Norwegian men's choruses.

A book cannot be written without the help of many others. These are the people I would like to thank: Indseth relatives - Thea Indseth, and Gail Indseth Stoick. Gail was a great help to me as I wrote the book.

I want to thank the Canton Public Library for letting me examine their files of old Canton newspapers, and glean information.

There are some people from Norway I want to acknowledge: My second-cousin, Odd Fladmark and his wife, Inger, found information for me in old census records, and they also put me in touch with Odd Williamsen, cultural sociologist/curator at the Nordmøre Museum in Kristiansund North. Williamsen was an immeasureable help to me in supplying needed input on the history and early life in Kristiansun. Also, I would like to thank Prof. Dr. h.c. Harald Herresthal of the Norwegian Academy of Music in Oslo, who also gave me necessary information.

I want to thank the persons who provided me with photographs; namely, the Indseth family, the Canton Public Library, Doris Harms, Hazel Larsgaard, Jerome Keiser and Donald Potraatz.

A special thanks to Gary Schultz who did the editing of my manuscript.

Chapter 1

*A*long the west coast of Norway, north of Bergen, north of Aalesund and north of Molde, lies the town of Kristiansund North. It is situated on three islands, with the Atlantic Ocean splashing at the islands' edges, and the towering Romsdal Mountains of the mainland for its eastern background.

Large ships always lay in her harbor, and a number of fishing boats also. Since the 1700's, these large ships have stopped here to take on their loads of lumber and *klippfisk* and deliver them to markets as far away as Spain, Germany, and South America.

Continually flying overhead are flocks of seagulls. Their coarse noises and loud screaming are a part of the everyday sounds.

The town of Kristiansund has long been the home of the *klippfisk* industry. This industry was the main source of employment in Kristiansund in the 1800's. *Klippfisk* warehouses were situated in many places on the islands. Fishermen brought in their catches of cod, but some was shipped in from as far north as Lofoten. Here in the warehouses in Kristiansund, the fish were cleaned, split, salted and laid out to dry until they were of a stiff cardboard consistency. The fish heads were clipped off so the product would fit the tin lined wooden boxes in which they were shipped. This food staple needed no refrigeration and was sent to markets in other parts of the world.

Klippfisk was a very special food in Kristiansund and Aalesund, but was not as common in the rest of Norway. Almost everyone in Kristiansund had some connection with the *klippfisk* industry, including a man named Rasmus Indseth.

Another day of work was finished and Rasmus Indseth and Ingebrigt Hanaseth left the fishy environment of the *klippfisk* warehouse and headed for home. As they neared their home on Bedehus Street, two children ran to meet them -- seven year old Andreas Indseth, the boy with the dark brown curly hair, and his three year old brother Hans. They each grabbed one of their father Rasmus' hands and escorted their father and his co-worker home.

Rasmus had built this house, #6A and #6B on Bedehus Street, alongside a row of other houses. This street got its name because the *bedehus* (or prayer house) was located there. Rasmus' house was in the town center, not far from the prison. The church was located at the city square, also not far away.

In 1865, Rasmus' house on Bedehus Street was home to seventeen persons. Besides Rasmus and his wife, Johanne Margrethe, seven of their children still lived at home. The rest of the people in the house were boarders. Rasmus' co-worker, Ingebrigt Hanaseth, and his wife, Elisabet, lived there, as well as fifty-six year old Petrine, who was on relief; Rasmus was paid from the *fattigkasse* (poor fund) for her keep. There was also a fisherman's widow, Marit Sivertsen, and her two teenage children, and twenty-two year old Marie, who was a seamstress, and the widow Anna. To earn a meager income, Anna and Marit carried firewood for others.

The house on Bedehus Street was of simple construction with many rooms of different sizes for the boarders. The large kitchen was used by all. This late afternoon the steam was rising from a huge kettle that hung over the fire in the kitchen fireplace. Today mother Johanne Indseth and Elisabet Hanaseth had prepared *sildball*. They had ground the raw potatoes, added barley flour and *spekesild* (dried salt herring) and shaped this mixture into balls. It took a large quantity to satisfy the appetites of seventeen hungry people. Now the balls of potatoes and sild were boiling in the water. This dish was a lot of work to prepare, but everyone was happy when it was on the menu. Soon this would be ready to eat, when the family and the boarders would sit down around the large table, pour melted butter over the *baller* and devour them. The people around the table, both young and old, were like one big family.

After the supper was finished and the boarders had gone to their rooms, Rasmus settled down in his *kubbestol* (wooden chair) to relax after the big meal. Little Hans climbed into his father's lap. Rasmus put his arm around his son, "Tell me, Hans Nicholai, have you been a good boy today?" His answer was a loud "*Ja!*", and then this little fellow's chubby arms went around his father's neck.

Now tousle-haired Andreas tugged at his father's sleeve. "*Pappa*, are you going to play your violin tonight?" Several times a week Rasmus got out his violin and entertained his family. He had never had lessons, but he could play many melodies. Often the family would sing along and harmonize.

After the musical session, when Rasmus began to put his violin and bow away, Andreas looked up at his father and timidly asked, "*Pappa*, could *I* play your violin?" To please his seven year old son, Rasmus' response was, "*Ja*, I suppose you can *try* it." He patiently helped position the violin under Andreas' chin, but when the boy took hold of the long bow and tried to pull it across the strings, he found it unwieldy.

Finally Rasmus shook his head and said, "*Nei*, Andreas, I think you are still too little to play the violin. We'll have to wait until you are older."

"*Someday* I am going to play the violin," Andreas emphatically informed his father. Rasmus believed him, for he had discovered that Andreas had an ear for music and was quick to catch on to melodies. When the town band played at the music pavilion in the park, or when it was marching in parades, Rasmus had noticed that Andreas was always there listening and enjoying music in all its forms. And Rasmus could understand this, because he had an ear for music too!

Little boys grow up, and seven years later, on June 7, 1872, Andreas celebrated his birthday. He now was fourteen years of age, had just finished *Folkeskole*, and had concluded his catechism training.

The last Sunday in June, 1872, was Confirmation Day at the Kristiansund Kirke. All the Indseth family had gathered there because Andreas was going to be confirmed. It was an important day in his life.

Like other churches along the coasts, a small boat hung from the ceiling above the pews, making those in attendance always aware of the need of God's protection for the fishermen and others on the sea.

The full sounds of the pipe organ brought the congregation to attention. This was an old church which had been built in 1725, and this church had the town's first pipe organ. It was from Holland with eight voices and a rotating star. A man, the *belgtrøer*, was situated behind the organ and pumped air for the organ.

A new organist had been secured this past year, Theodor Hilde, and he was the music man in Kristiansund now, as previous organists had been. Besides the tasks at the church, he directed the town band, taught a choir at school, and gave music lessons – vocal, and instrumental, including the organ. Andreas had been in Hilde's school choir this past year.

Andreas listened to the pipe organ music, and he thought, "*This is what I would like to do – play the organ and teach music, like Mr. Hilde.*"

After the hymn was finished and the lingering chords of the pipe organ faded, the black-robed *Prest* (Pastor) climbed up the steps into the pulpit. He was a stern looking man. His beard hung over the front of his stiff wide, white accordion-like collar. He looked over the congregation, paused, and then cleared his throat. Now he spoke directly to the thirteen and fourteen year old confirmands.

"My dear friends, today you are starting a new phase in your lives. This is a special day for you." Here he paused.

"Now you have progressed from childhood to adulthood.

"What does that mean, you ask? It is that you are old enough now to make decisions. You have finished this part of your schooling and your catechism training, and now you must decide what to do with your life. Should you find a job...and learn a trade? Or perhaps a few of you will go on to *Gymnasium* school. Yes, there are some big decisions for you to make now."

The pastor looked directly into the faces of the young people to whom he was speaking, and went on. "I want to tell you that today there is an even more important decision you must make. That is why we are here! Now you are old enough. Today you must make a *spiritual* decision."

The pastor stopped a moment, then forcefully went on. "Don't think this is just a routine we go through which is only taking place in this church building!"

To emphasize his words, he now pounded the pulpit.

"No! I want to tell you something.... *Heaven is watching and listening!*

"If from your hearts you say,... and mean what you say,... up in heaven today there will be rejoicing when each one of you says, '*Yes!*'"

Now the black-robed *Prest* had finished his confirmation sermon. He quietly bowed his head, closed his eyes and stood for a moment as if in prayer. When he raised his head, he made this pronouncement "*May heaven have something to celebrate today!*"

The *klokker* announced the next hymn, and the *belgtrøer* began to pump air for the organ, yet the congregation remained quiet. Today the *Prest* had given everyone – not only the confirmands - something to think about.

Soon the chords from the organ filled the church and the people joined in song.

After the service, the family returned to the house on *Bedehus* Street. While mother Johanne Margrethe and her older daughters prepared *middag* (dinner), the men of the family gathered outside by the front door. It was a lovely midsummer day, a day to enjoy the out-of-doors.

"Come on out, Andreas," his father called. "You are included with the men now!"

Today Rasmus' oldest son, John Adolph, and his wife, Mildri, had joined them. John Adolph was a master baker now and worked at a bakery in Kristiansund.

Rasmus addressed his young son, "Well, Andreas, did you hear what the Pastor had to say today about making decisions? Have you thought about what you are going to do next?"

Everyone was curious to know what he would say. Andreas slowly ran his fingers through his thick curly hair, and finally made this statement:

"*I want to be a music teacher*. I want to take music lessons so I can play in the town band, and play the violin ....and someday I want to play the organ!"

"You'll need money if you are going to do all this," his father said.

"I talked to organist Hilde at choir practice last week about joining the town band, and he said there was a cornet I could buy very cheap, and I could start lessons right away."

"Andreas, you can't live just on music. You should learn a trade so you can make a living." As an afterthought, his father added, "I could get you a job at the *klippfisk* warehouse."

"John Adolph just told me that he thought he could get me a job at the bakery where he works," Andreas quickly replied.

Andreas turned to his older brother for confirmation. "You said they needed a *bakery boy*, didn't you?"

"Yes, a bakery boy was how I began!"

His brother then added, "But I warn you, Andreas, you will have to get up very early every morning!"

Father Rasmus had been silent as he considered all of this.

When he continued, it was with enthusiasm, "Well, Andreas, this might work out very well. The bakery day begins before dawn, so you will be finished with your job in early afternoon and then you'll have time to practice, and work on your music.......*and you will have money for your lessons too*!"

Rasmus continued nodding his head in agreement to what he had just said, and added, "I will be happy for you, Andreas, if you can get training in your music. I never had a chance to learn to read notes."

"It sounds to me like you're interested in working in the bakery, Andreas," his older brother said, "so you'd better come down to the bakery tomorrow and see Mr. Petersen before someone else gets the job!"

Inger Meilke (Indseth) - 1876

Chapter 2

*E*rnst Petersen's Bakery was filled with delicious smells of baking bread and cinnamon and cardamom. Andreas now had been working for over two months as a *bakerdreng* (bakery boy) there. His brother, John Adolph, was by his side to advise and explain his duties.

Andreas had finally learned the correct process when providing wood for the large oven. First, the oven must be very hot for the little fancy rolls which were baked first, and then he had to drop the temperature a little, but keep it steady while the loaves of bread were baking. He must know how many pieces of firewood to add to produce the right heat for the oven.

Andreas also was the errand boy, getting supplies, and doing odd jobs. Each day Andreas could enjoy these delicious baking odors. He thought about how fortunate he was to not have to work in the fishy climate amid the smells of the *klippfisk* warehouses.

Today two of Rasmus' boarders, Elisabet and Marie, were making a trip to Kristiansund's shops. Marie needed thread for the dress on which she was working, and Elisabet planned to buy some yarn. It was time to start knitting mittens, she told Marie. Winter would soon be here, and she liked to help Johanne Margrethe furnish mittens for her large family.

This lovely September morning, the bread-baking aroma even wafted out into the street.

"Smells like the baking is finished for today," Elisabet commented. "Let's stop and look in the window and see what is available today."

The two ladies leaned up to the display window.

"Oh, they made the rolls with that prune and cream filling today! They're delicious, and my Ingebrigt's favorite."

"And there's *skillingsboller* too!" Marie pointed to the large round anise flavored loaves.

8

And there were many loaves of bread, both rye and wheat.

Then Andreas, dressed in a white baker's coat, came to the window with a tray of fresh doughnuts. He and John Adolph had just finished frying them.

"I wonder how Andreas likes his job by now," Marie spoke, but this was the question on both of their minds.

"Those *smultringer* (doughnuts) look so good," Elisabet said, "why don't we buy some to take back to the house? We'll make some coffee and get Johanne Margrethe to sit down for a few minutes and have some coffee and doughnuts. I think her youngest should be napping now."

Rasmus and Johanne Margrethe Indseth had been adding to their family. They now had another John – John August, who was two years old; Joachim, who was seven years; and a daughter, Anna, all three younger than Hans Nicholai.

"Petrine should be up from her afternoon nap by now. I'm sure she'd like Andreas' doughnuts too!"

After Andreas had helped with the cleaning in the baking room and had put the supplies away, he headed for home. Under his arms were some loaves of day-old bread that Petersen had sent home with him. It was a pleasant September afternoon and he headed home to practice his cornet. Mr. Hilde had told him he had now progressed enough to attend the town band practice that night.

When Spring came, the outside activities resumed. The green leaves were coming out on the birch trees, and the grass was now covering the ground where the snow had been. It was time for the town band to give a concert in the music pavilion in the park.

Today Andreas lovingly lifted his band cap from his head, admired it, and set it back in place again. He was excited. This was the first time he had dressed in his band uniform. In his hand was his cornet, and he was ready to join the rest of the band. First, he would march with the town band in the parade. Afterwards they would give a concert in the park.

When the band arrived at the pavilion, Mr. Hilde lifted his baton, and the music began. Andreas carefully counted out the beats so he would come in with his cornet at the right time. He enjoyed the music as the sounds from his horn blended with the rest of the band instruments and made pleasing harmony. Today he was part of the music! And, to top it off, there was an audience out there. From time to time he glanced at them and noticed that they were enjoying it. There was something about band music with its lively beat that almost made a person want to get up and march. Band music had a way of bringing out enthusiasm and emitting energy. Today was Andreas' first concert, and he was enjoying it.

"Andreas, I've got some news for you!" Rasmus was home from work, and his son, Andreas, was soon at his side.

"Today one of the men at the warehouse mentioned that his neighbor had a violin that he was anxious to sell. It seems his neighbor had been fortunate enough to locate one of Lars Hoem's violins."

Rasmus paused, and then explained that Lars Hoem had been Kristiansund's own famous violin maker. "Lars Hoem made five hundred violins, did you know that, Andreas? And guitars too."

A French master on an English prison-ship in Plymouth, England, during the Napoleon Wars, back between 1809 and 1814, had taught Hoem. They both had been war prisoners. Afterwards, Hoem had come to Kristiansund and made violins and guitars.

Continuing with his news, Rasmus went on, "Well, my co-worker's neighbor purchased this special violin that Lars Hoem had made, and now he wants to sell his own violin at a very reasonable price. I know you would like your own violin, so do you think we should check it out?"

"Oh yes, *Pappa*! I'd really like a violin." His heart began to beat faster. "Then I can start violin lessons also."

"Andreas, you must remember that it takes one day of your wages to pay for one lesson."

Andreas did some quick figuring in his head, "But *Pappa*, with only one lesson each week on the violin, and one on the cornet, I'll still have four days' wages to spend each week. I should have some money left to purchase the violin."

"*Ja, vel*, I already told my co-worker to mention to his neighbor that we were interested."

Three years later, in 1875, Andreas was still working in Ernst Petersen's Bakery. His time still was spent between the bakery and his music.

The organist, Mr. Hilde, had left Kristiansund for another position, and now Andreas had no music teacher, but he was determined to continue with his practicing. He knew he had to keep his lip in shape.

After work, on a nice July day, he took his cornet and went for a walk. In the large meadow behind the house, he found his favorite large rock, and sat down. There was green grass all around, and even some wild flowers blooming here and there. He was close to the sea, and could hear the lapping sound of the waves splashing against the rocks. Looking to the east, the mighty mountains, *Reinsfjellet, Tustnastabben* and *Freikollen*, stood as guards over the town. Above the water's edge, the white seagulls gathered in their erratic flight, uttering their loud coarse noises. They were part of this familiar environment.

In competition to the seagulls, Andreas picked up his cornet, and put it to his lips. Mr. Hilde in his lessons had given him several pieces to memorize, and he began to play, all the while critiquing his cornet's tones. He was pleased because today even the high notes came out clear.

When he stopped, he discovered the seagulls had moved on. From a tree by the water's edge came a little twittering sound. Where he was sitting, he could see the little *meis* (titmouse) on a branch. He listened and smiled. Yes, every bird has a song, some more pleasing than others. In fact, he had discovered that if you are listening, you can hear the sound of music coming from all of nature.

1876 brought the new church organist to town. He was a highly qualified musician and an excellent organist and violinist. He had studied in Christiania and Brussels, Belgium. His name was Christian Braein. He had grown up outside of Lillehammer and spoke with the dialect of Gudbrandsdalen. Mr. Braein was a man of average height, slim build, and balding, with just a medium-sized tuft of hair on top. He was a pleasant and hard-working man.

Mr. Braein soon had the musical organizations going again – the town band and the town orchestra. Andreas Indseth joined both, and he began lessons from Mr. Braein on the organ and violin.

One day Andreas came home from his organ lesson and reported to his parents that one of Mr. Braein's teachers in Christiania had been the famed organist and composer, Ludvig Mathias Lindeman.

"Mr. Braein will use one of Lindeman's compositions in church on Sunday. He played that hymn on the organ for me today. It's '*Kirken den er et gammelt hus*' (Built on a Rock the Church Doth Stand). It was powerful. Mr. Braein had all the stops out!"

Andreas' father commented that Kristiansund Kirke was fortunate to have such an educated musician as Mr. Braein.

"What about it, Andreas? Won't you soon be finished with all these lessons?"

"Oh, no! There is so much to learn. Music is not just being able to read notes. Did you know that the cornet cannot play from the same music as the other instruments? The music must be transposed into b flat; therefore, I'll have to learn how to transpose.

"...and if I am to play music the way the composer wrote it, I must learn the *musical* meaning of all those Italian words – *pianissimo, fortissimo, staccato, crescendo, allegretto*, and more.

"and counting out the time with quarter notes, sixteenth notes, thirty-second notes and rests and holds, sometimes gets very confusing."

His father shook his head. "It sounds too complicated to me."

Andrew added, "I'll also need vocal lessons if I am to be a music teacher and lead choirs some day."

Andreas' looks had been changing. He still had his thick dark brown hair with its tendency to curl, but now he had grown a mustache and a stylish beard. He no longer looked like an adolescent. He had grown into a man both in his actions and his looks. He now was tall in stature and walked with an erect posture. He was eighteen years old, had a job, and he had a goal.

Mr. Braein had organized a choir, and Andreas and his brother, Hans, became a part of it. Andreas had a fine baritone voice and was also taking vocal training from Mr. Braein.

Another member of the choir was a girl named Inger Meilke. She had a lovely coloratura soprano voice. Andreas and Hans Nicholai were in the habit of walking her home after choir practice.

Inger had been orphaned when both her parents died while she was only a little girl. For most of her life she had been living with another family. Her brother had worked on a fishing boat, but he had been lost at sea. Inger was sixteen years old.

As Inger and Andreas became better acquainted, soon it was only Andreas who walked Inger home after choir practice.

Inger was a rather quiet person, with striking looks, and lovely blue eyes. Her dark hair was parted in the middle, drawn back from her face, and arranged in a bun in the back. She often wore tiny ringlets around her face. Inger had a cameo-like profile, with a regal nose. She had an interest in music also. Besides her lovely voice, she played the guitar, and, best of all, she was always encouraging Andreas in his music.

Wedding Photo - 1878
Andreas and Inger Indseth

Chapter 3

*A*ndreas was progressing rapidly with his music. Mr. Braein was a good teacher who tried to cover all the basics of music that he felt Andreas needed. He challenged Andreas with one difficult piece of music after another. Andreas was becoming very proficient on the violin, his favorite instrument, as well as the organ and cornet.

Mr. Braein was concerned about each of his pupils and their progress. As Andrew got to know Mr. Braein, he discovered that he had a sense of humor, and he also noticed that Mr. Braein could get very emotional over music. Mr. Braein was always working on material for the frequent concerts that he had for his choirs, band and orchestra.

A new Kristiansund church was built in 1878 on Kirkelandet Island. A pipe organ with nineteen voices was obtained for it from Rieger and Sohne Schlesien, of Germany. Andreas and his brother Hans were fortunate to be able to take their organ lessons and do their practicing on the new organ.

In the fall of 1878, after almost two years of lessons, Mr. Braein gave Andreas something to think about. "Andreas, I feel it is time for you to move on. I can give you the names of some fine music teachers in Christiania. I feel that you need to get into the musical environment there. You are now twenty years old. In Christiania you can join choirs, bands and orchestras. You'll discover that the members of these groups there, with advanced training, are on a different level musically than the members of the town band and orchestra here in Kristiansund. In Christiania you can attend concerts and recitals, along with your lessons. This all will give you a well-rounded basis if you are going to be a music teacher."

Although Hans Nicholai was four years younger than Andreas, and now only sixteen, in two years of lessons, he was also ready to go forward. Mr. Braein also gave Hans the names of some excellent organ teachers in Christiania.

Andreas and Hans Nicholai were excited at the prospect of life and music in Christiania and began to make plans. They decided to spend Christmas with their family and then make their move to the big city the beginning of the new year of 1879.

Andreas had to share his plans with Inger. She listened intently, and was very happy for him, but after hearing all the details, she sadly remarked, "Christiania is so far from Kristiansund, Andreas. I'll miss you."

That gave Andreas something more to consider.

When Christmas had come and gone, Andreas and Hans Nicholai stood on the kai (quay) in Kristiansund, where the ship was loading. They had their suitcases, and Andreas had his violin and cornet. Many members of their family were there to see them off - their father and mother, and their younger brothers, John August and Joachim, and younger sister Anna.

Christmas this year had held a special event. It seemed that the more Andreas thought about being separated from Inger, the more determined he became to take her along, and they had decided to get married. Andreas had realized that what Inger had said was true....*that Kristiansund was so far from Christiania that they would never get to see each other.* So today Inger was there also, with her suitcases. She was no longer Inger Meilke, but now, at age seventeen, she carried the Indseth name.

The three Indseth passengers went aboard, and the noisy ship pulled out of the Kirstiansund harbor, heading south. They stood on the deck and watched as the town of Kristiansund receded, and the white winterclad mountains in the background finally disappeared. Soon all they could see was the sea, but from time to time islands would appear along the coast. The ship would sail along the western coast of Norway and around the southern tip and then head north until it reached the harbor of Christiania, a long voyage. Kristiansund, their home town, had no railroad, so most of the travel from that town was done by ship.

Each of the three passengers' thrill at this adventure was tinged with a bit of concern for the future, but Andreas and Inger assured each other that things would work out.

* * * * *

Oh, the excitement and bustle of the big city compared to Kristiansund with its mere seven or eight thousand population!

The first thing on Andreas' mind was to find a job. With his experience as a baker, he soon found one in a bakery. This would give him most of his afternoons for lessons and practice.

Now with all the musical opportunities here, Andreas had to choose which ones would fit into his free time, and which ones were his highest priorities. He quickly joined an orchestra and band, and a men's chorus.

He shared his goals with Inger. "I need to learn more about bands so I will be able to teach every instrument, and I also should be able to arrange their music. I will need lessons in music theory and composition." Then he added, "I want piano lessons! Aside from the pleasing sounds of the violin, and the organ, I want to be able to play the lively music of the piano. I'd like to be able to perform some of Edvard Grieg's piano compositions. I've heard some of them and yearn to play them for myself. Besides, by studying the piano, I'll be able to be an accompanist, which is necessary if one is in the music field."

Inger made it sound so simple, "Just take each step as things open up for you, Andreas."

Their lives were full of music and happiness. They attended choir concerts and band concerts and recitals. The music at these events often stirred Andreas so much that on the way home from concerts his spirits were high. He would be very excited as he recalled and raved about the musical moments that touched him. Sometimes it was the melody, and sometimes he was affected by the way the instruments were featured in the pieces. Or when he was listening to choruses, it could be the harmony, or a solo, or a certain refrain.

Andreas was recognizing in himself the same trait he had discovered in Mr. Braein – that of *becoming emotional over music.*

Since arriving in Christiania, Andreas had met other young men who had the same musical ambitions that he had. Even over a coffee cup, the conversations of Andreas and his friends were about music.

In their second year in Christiania, Inger gave birth, but all didn't go well. The baby only lived a short time. They named the baby Ingvald. This was a shock to both Andreas and Inger, but it affected Inger much more than Andreas, who was busy with his music. By now, Andreas had given up his bakery job, and for income, he was giving lessons on the violin and cornet. His young students addressed him as Professor Indseth. But for Inger what she had been looking forward to had suddenly become days of emptiness.

"What happened to your smile, Inger?" Andreas gently questioned her one day. "I miss it." He sat down beside her.

"This has been hard for you, I know." Andreas put his arm around her. "It hurt me to lose our little boy too." Now Inger let her bottled-up feelings gush out, and the tears flowed.

"Before our Ingvald was born, I was looking forward to his birth, and to days when I could hold our little baby in my arms...."

Inger stopped to wipe the tears from her eyes, and then she finished her sentence ".... and loving him."

She turned to Andreas as she spoke. "Now, I catch myself still waiting for something, but then I ask myself... '*waiting for what?*' My days are so empty."

Inger paused as her thoughts went back to her baby. "I'll always remember him with his dark hair... Some day I think it would have been curly just like yours!"

Again the sadness came into her voice, "What was part of me several weeks ago, now lies in a grave." She began to sob.

"Just cry, Inger. Let it come out." He pulled her close, laying her head against his chest. He gently stroked her hair.

Andreas quietly shared with her. "Several days ago I came across some music. The melody has been running through my head ever since and the words have helped me." He softly began to sing to her....

	(translation)
"*Velt alle dine veier*	Leave all your ways
og all din hjertesorg	and all your heartaches
paa ham som evig eier	with Him who from eternity holds
den hele himlens borg....	all of heaven's powers;
Han som kan stormen binde	He who can still the storm
og bryte bolgen blaa,	and calm the waves of blue,
Han skal og veien finne,	He shall find a way,
den vei hvor du kan gaa."	a way for you to go.

Inger snuggled up to him. It was a tender moment for them both. "*I love you, Inger*," Andreas whispered.

Then he added, "Perhaps God will give us another child."

Andreas was enjoying his work of teaching. Most of his students were young and were beginners on their instruments. "Now when they see me on the street, they call me *Professor* Indseth," he told Inger. Andreas was pleased to see his students' progress.

For several months the orchestra of which Andreas was a member had been practicing for a special event. The King of Sweden was coming to Christiania. At this time he was also the King of Norway. It was a grand occasion, and for Andreas it was a once-in-a-lifetime opportunity. Here in Christiania, there were so many exciting musical events happening. To perform for royalty was an unforgettable experience for Andreas. He would always remember that he had played his violin for a King.

Andreas attended as many concerts and recitals as he could. This way he learned of new music and became acquainted with some of the musicians in the musical world of Christiania. Often a group of musicians would gather afterwards and visit over a cup of coffee. In these gatherings Andreas met an Alexander Bull, son of the famous violinist, Ole Bull. At this time Alexander was living in France and working with about six musicians, setting up concerts for them, and later following with them to European cities to take care of all of the details. Alexander was in Christiania often, and Andreas and Alexander became friends.

One night Alexander Bull told of his trip to America when his father was on a concert tour there. To Andreas, this man was a very interesting person, especially when he found out that Alexander was a violinist also; this gave them something in common.

On May 3, 1882, Inger and Andreas were blessed with a healthy baby girl. Inez Amanda put joy into Inger's life again.

Later that summer, Andreas received a letter from Kristiansund from his baker brother, John Adolph.

Dear Andreas,

  I suppose you often wonder how things are here in Kristiansund. I must tell you that Mother and Father are well. Also the rest of the family. My girls are growing up and they send their greetings.

  The latest news is that I have my own bakery now. It is on Langveien #25 here in Kristiansund. I'm rather proud of it. I could give you a job if you were here in Kristiansund now. But I understand you are doing what you love to do, being involved with your music. Now our younger brothers, Joachim, and John August, are getting involved in music too, with Joachim on the violin, and both singing in choirs.

  Greet Inger, and Hans, and congratulations on your baby girl!

Your brother,

John Adolph and Mildri

Exactly two years after baby Inez was born, on May 3, 1884, Inger gave birth to a son, Reinhart. Andreas was proud to have both a son and a daughter, and Inger now was a busy mother.

About this time, one of the churches in the suburbs of Christiania hired Andreas as their church organist. He was to fill in until their next organist would be able to arrive.

Andreas enjoyed this assignment. He now had a church choir, band, and private music lessons, besides the organist duties. Andreas was conscientious and really, in the back of his mind, he was using what his teacher, Mr. Braein, had taught him. Mr. Braein was his model as to how these various jobs should be done.

Andreas was always looking for new pieces of organ music to use in the Sunday service. And his aim in working with the choir was to draw out beautiful harmony from the singers' voices, and to insist that the words of the message they sang were understandable.

Chapter 4

*J*n Norway, in the 1880's, there was what was called *America fever.* Thousands of Norwegians were leaving their native land for America. The steamship lines were advertising their voyages to America. They had agents all over Norway who were selling tickets, and helping the travelers at the ports.

Some Norwegians who had emigrated to America were now coming back to visit in Norway with reports of how successful they had become. America was pictured as the land of opportunities. *Going to America* was the topic of conversations everywhere. Andreas and Inger knew of a number of families who had left.

Brother Hans Nicholai left Christiania in August of 1884 to attend the *Klaebu Seminary* near Trondhjem, Norway. Besides being a church organist, he wanted teacher's training. Hans would study there for two years.

In 1885, Andreas took a music teacher position at Bodø. Bodø was a town in northern Norway, on the coast north of Kristiansund, and was, in fact, the first coastal town within the Arctic Circle.

In the process of moving from Christiania to Bodø, the family stopped in Kristiansund for a few days. Andreas' father, Rasmus, was now bedridden, an old man of almost seventy years. Several of the grandchildren were living with them and helping his mother with the care of his father.

Rasmus was so happy to see Andreas and his little family. Visiting with Andreas, he mentioned, "Lying here day after day, there is something I have been longing for."

"What is that, *Pappa*?" Andreas asked.

" It's the sound of the violin!" he said. "Do you suppose you could get my old violin down and play some tunes for me?"

Andreas was more than happy to fulfill his request. He picked up the old violin and gently caressed it. It brought back memories of days past when it was his father that had held it and brought joy to him and the rest of the family. It was his father's interest in music that had encouraged him to become involved with the violin, organ and cornet.

Andreas tightened up the strings of the instrument and tuned it. It had not been played for some time. When Andreas drew the bow across the strings, his father closed his eyes, enjoying the sound of a light-hearted melody.

Then his father had one more request, "Now let me hear one of your *educated* pieces!"

Andreas played a portion of one of Paganini's compositions, and both Andreas and his father reveled in this complicated melody. The many difficult parts displayed to Rasmus his son's abilities. When he finished, his father lay back on the pillow, closed his eyes and softly announced, "*Ja*, that was music!"

* * * * *

Andreas was a busy man, as director of the choir and *musikk korps* (brass band), and as music teacher in Bodø. He was anxious to get a *Mandskor* (men's chorus) started there. He had sung in a men's chorus in Christiania, and now these men's choruses were becoming very popular and were being started all over Norway. Andreas was drawn to the pleasing sound of the rich blending of men's voices. He worked diligently with this men's group to encourage and train them. He found arrangements that brought pleasing harmony. This organization soon became very popular. Their concerts were very well attended, and they received much acclaim.

One day towards the end of January, 1887, almost two years after their Kristiansund visit, a letter arrived from Andreas' mother.

> **Dear Andreas,**
>
> **Den Dag, Den Sorg! (Each day has its own sorrows.) Pappa passed away January 18th. All of the family who lives near here gathered for the funeral, but it was a very cold, wintery day, and the snow was blowing.**
>
> **It was a sad day.**
>
> **Ja, that's the way it is! I want you to know that you brought much joy to your father on your last visit.**
>
> > **Love,**
> > **Mother**

A sadness came over Andreas. The man who had loved him and who had encouraged him, and who had passed along his love for music was gone. "Did I ever thank him? Why didn't I tell him the last time we were in Kristiansund?" Andreas finally decided, "I will have to thank him by continuing with my music and bringing musical enjoyment to others."

After a concert of the Bodø Mandskor in 1887, when Andreas himself was proud and very satisfied with his group's performance, a man approached Andreas to compliment him and his chorus. This man was visiting his relatives in Bodø. He went on and on about how he wished they could have a men's chorus in Dakota Territory in America where he lived. He suggested, "Professor Indseth, why don't you come over and help us get some music started in Sioux Falls?"

Andreas had a long visit with him. This man explained that the children of the pioneers, these second generation of Norwegian immigrants, hadn't had an opportunity to be trained in music because in those early days on the prairie there were no music teachers. He emphasized that there were many little Norwegian communities north and south of Sioux Falls. These had been settled by Norwegians and now their children were growing up, and they yearned for music. They wanted choirs and bands. "This would be a wonderful opportunity for you, Professor Indseth!"

Andreas thanked him for applauding his chorus, but at that time he didn't even consider this man's idea. He had a good job, and his little family had been growing. In April of 1886, their third child, Andreas Kristian, Jr., had been born. He had responsibilities here, with a wife and three children.

Perhaps if he had been a single man, he would have considered it. It certainly would be a challenge to bring music to an area, especially when people longed for it.

Chapter 5

*I*nger opened the large trunk and began to place articles in it. She had several lovely woolen pieces which she had woven, and some hardanger-embroidered cloths she had made. The large silver spoons given them for their wedding with their initials engraved on the back, together with the set of small coffee spoons, she tucked into one corner. On the floor lay things she had been gathering to pack in the trunk. Here was her special rolling pin. She would need that to make *lefse* and *flatbrød*. She must take along blankets and clothes for the children. Her *Nordmøre bunad* (costume) had to be packed.

Inger picked up baby Jennie Margaret's long white baptismal gown with the tiny tucks and the white embroidery, and the cap that went with it. Last summer before her last child had been born she had spent many hours working on the elaborate embroidery, and sewing the dainty garment together. She was careful with it as she gently folded it and laid it in the trunk.

Little Jennie would already be one year old in a couple of months. She had been born July 10, 1888. She was Andreas and Inger's fourth child.

Andreas came into the room and stood watching Inger. He reminded her, "You must leave space for my violin, cornet and baton. And I will need the black suit I use when conducting; also, there are some music books I want to take along."

Andreas and Inger had caught the *America fever*. They now had tickets to sail for America in two weeks - May 3, 1889.

It all had started about two years ago when the man from Sioux Falls spoke to Andreas about the need for music teachers in his part of America. At first, Andreas had hardly dared to speak to Inger about this issue, because he wasn't certain how he himself felt about making such a big move. When he did, Inger only pointed out, "You are the one who must decide if we should leave. Your mother is still living here, and all your brothers and sisters. I have no relatives in Norway. Our own family, we will take them with us."

Andreas and Inger discussed and debated the pros and cons...and then a letter came from America. The man from Sioux Falls asked Andreas to seriously consider coming there, and he offered to help him get settled when they arrived. After that letter, Andreas began checking on the various steamship lines and the ticket prices. The Allan Line was the one they decided on. This would take them from Trondhjem, Norway, to Quebec, Canada, and from there they would go on to Detroit and Sioux Falls. They were now in the process of selling their furniture and the other belongings that they couldn't take with them.

Andreas got out the steamship company's pamphlet, and reread the information there to Inger. "Here it says .....

> 9 a.m. – The breakfasts will consist of tea, coffee, hot chocolate, sugar, bread and butter, and biscuits and butter.
> 1 p.m. – Dinners will consist of soup, meat and potatoes, and on Sunday plum pudding will be served.
> 6 p.m. – Suppers will consist of tea, coffee, hot chocolate, sugar, bread and butter, and biscuits and butter."

Inger interrupted him, "We will have to take a lunch basket along. The children may not like the ship's food. We can take some *flatbrød* and *geitost* (goat cheese), and some apples for them to lunch on. Maybe when we stop in Kristiansund we can buy some loaves of John Adolph's good bread from his bakery. Good bread and cheese will always satisfy the children. I don't know what this ship bread will be like. It may be hard and dry."

Andreas continued reading –

> "Bring a large pail to be used for water, which your family will need for drinking and washing."

".....and here are the rules:

> "Smoking can be done only on the deck. You are expected to attend services on the deck on Sunday and be dressed in a clean manner to honor the Sabbath. If you have alcoholic beverages along, you must leave them in the Captain's possession, and they will be doled out sparingly. Everyone is expected to be in bed at 10 p.m."

Andreas added, "I guess these rules are needed to keep order when there are hundreds of third-class passengers on board."

The first stop for Andreas and Inger and their family on their journey to America was Andreas' hometown of Kristiansund. They spent several days there with Andreas' mother, Johanne Margrethe. They were surprised to see how her health had failed. Now she was very frail, and not feeling well. "*I am so tired*," she told them. They were glad they had stopped, but this parting was harder than any other because Andreas knew it was a final farewell. There were good-byes to brother, John Adolph, and Andreas' sisters also.

Andreas' two younger brothers, Joachim and John August, had moved to Christiania to further their musical careers, and Hans was back in Christiania again. He had married a young lady named Beret, and was a school master at Grefsen School, and an organist at Vestre Aker Church.

As the ship pulled out of the harbor of Kristiansund on May 1, Andreas stood on the deck with his oldest son, five-year-old Reinhart. They watched as the town slowly disappeared in the fog. Andreas' eyes longingly searched the last vistas of this town of his birth and of his youth until everything disappeared altogether. It would be the last time he saw Kristiansund.

They were instructed to be in Trondhjem a day before sailing to get their baggage marked and ready for loading, and to fill out all the papers necessary for emigrating. The next stop would be England. Sailing day, May 3, came and the Indseth family departed from Trondhjem and their native land of Norway.

By the second day of their voyage, the ship reached the North Sea, bringing seasickness to many. Inger became very seasick. "I feel awful. Don't even talk to me," she told Andreas. She gave baby Jennie to him and went to bed. Seven-year-old Inez Amanda didn't feel well either, and she also went to bed. For a couple of days Andreas had three children in his care - one-year-old baby Jennie, three-year-old Andreas, Jr., and five-year-old Reinhart.

Andreas had his hands full feeding them, and keeping them in tow. He discovered how busy Inger was every day. When night came he was anxious to get them to bed, and this is how he did it: After supper each night, he gathered them around him, with the two youngest on his lap and Reinhart sitting at his feet, and he would sing them to sleep. Their favorite lullaby was "*Det var en deilig, deilig dag.*" (It was a lovely, lovely day.)

His sleepy song was about the lovely day that had come to an end, and now it was time for all who were very good to go to sleep.

He would sing to them about the flower-buds that no longer turned their faces towards the sun. Now they were tired too, poor little things, and closed their petals so they could sleep a while.

He sang about the little white lambs that now lay in the barn. His song described how they would snuggle up to their brothers....and then Andreas would put his finger to his lips and whisper, "*Shhhh! The lambs are going to sleep!*"

Andreas would repeat the verse about the lovely day that had now come to an end when all who were very good would be fast asleep. Now the stars looked down and twinkled for they were very happy when they saw the little flowers with their petals closed, the lambs at rest, and sleeping little girls and boys.

The children usually were so tired, that before he was finished with all the verses, they all would be asleep.

After reaching Hull, England, they were transferred to Liverpool and sailed for America from there. The Atlantic voyage of eight days went well. When the weather was good, the family spent a lot of time on deck to get the fresh air. Many of the eight hundred third class passengers were young people, and there was always dancing on the deck. One day there was a service for a man who had died. It was sad to see the wooden coffin thrown into the sea.

What excitement when the first sight of land was discovered! Before long, Andreas and Inger and their family landed safely in Quebec, and then on to Detroit and Sioux Falls. Inger couldn't wait until she could stand on solid ground again. "I am no seaman," she confessed.

It was a group of weary people who got off the train in Sioux Falls, Dakota Territory. It had been almost three weeks since they had left Norway and they were all tired and dirty from traveling, but they were happy to have finally reached their destination.

Andreas looked around at the crowd of people waiting to meet passengers, and there he was! Andreas recognized him as the Mr. Christiansen he had visited with in Bodø, the man who had written to him.

"Professor Indseth? the man asked.

"*Ja,,*" answered Andreas.

"May I call you Andrew?" he inquired.

Andreas then realized that Christiansen was addressing him with the American version of his name.

"Andrew, I am taking you and your family home with us for a few days until you have time to get settled."

They loaded their suitcases in the back of the buggy. "We'll come back later and get your big trunk," he said.

When they got to Mr. Christiansen's home in Sioux Falls, his wife, Ragna, welcomed them. "I'm sure the first thing you want to do is wash up," she said. "Here are towels and soap and you can use our tub."

Then she emphatically added, *"but bring all of your dirty clothes to the basement.* We'll wash them with strong soap and hang them outside in the sunshine. Perhaps there are little bugs hiding in them. We have had newcomers staying with us before, and you never know what they bring along from the ship."

She came with clean clothes for everyone. Many of the garments were too large, but these were clean and after bathing, these felt so good on their clean bodies. Having clean hair felt good too.

Ragna Christiansen looked at their woolen garments. "Mrs. Indseth, you will need some cooler clothes for the children and yourself. The next few months may be very hot around here, and these woolen clothes will be most uncomfortable."

Ragna wanted to be helpful. "Here is what we will do. In a few days after you find a place to live, I'll go with you and we will buy some calico and cotton cloth and I'll help you sew garments for the children and yourself. I have a machine that sews, and I have a neighbor lady who I know will help us. She is from north Norway also."

Inger didn't feel like a stranger in this new country when this kindly woman was offering to help her with her needs. Ragna was an efficient, motherly person and Inger felt she had found a friend.

The next day Christiansen and Andrew went looking for furnished rooms. "Your family can live in these rooms to start with, and then you can take your time looking for a house and buying some furniture."

"Mr. Christiansen, I will need a job until I can get acquainted and learn the language so I can teach music. On the train I discovered what it was like to have people speak to me in a foreign language."

Then Andrew asked him, "Tell me, are there any bakeries in Sioux Falls that are run by Norwegians? I've had experience as a baker."

"Don't worry, Andrew. There are several bakeries you can contact; *some even bake Norwegian delicacies*! And as to the language, I can assure you that there are many Norwegians living in this community with whom you and your family can speak Norwegian. You'll find out that you will absorb the new language as you mix with other English-speaking people. Won't one of your children be starting school this fall?"

"*Ja*, our oldest, Inez Amanda, is seven now and old enough for school."

"Well, she'll learn it first, and then soon you all will be speaking English! There are many from Norway living here and soon you'll get acquainted...... and maybe soon we can start *singing* together. I'm looking forward to that!"

Chapter 6

*T*he scenery of Norway was only a memory for Andrew and Inger now. They couldn't help noticing the difference in this landscape of the Dakotas. Here there were no mountains, no harbors, no boats. Not even any seagulls! Besides that, Dakota Territory in the year of 1889 had a drought. The weather was hot and dry.

Here the land lay so flat, Andrew and Inger could see for miles and miles, but they discovered that against the flat western horizon, they often would see some beautiful sunsets.

The first mail Andrew received in America was from his older brother, John Adolph, from Kristiansund. Andrew opened the envelope and began to read...

> **Dear brother,**
> **I must tell you that our mother passed away on May 5th,**
> **only four days after you were here.**

Andrew re-read that sentence, laid down the letter, and called, "Inger, come here!"

When she sat down at the table with him, Andrew quietly announced, "*Mother is dead!*"

"I'm so sorry, *Andreas*," Inger sympathized.

"I knew this was coming when we were there," Andrew said. "I had a feeling she didn't have much time left. *Dear Mother*. She was such a hard worker, caring for all of us children, and cooking for boarders for many years. It was a hard life for her."

Andrew sat and let thoughts of his mother flood his mind.

"She always had time for us. Do you know what memories come back to me now? I remember as a little boy how she put us to bed every night. Even if she was tired, she always had time for each of us. As we knelt by our beds, she stood there and listened to our prayers. It was a nightly custom."

Inger was impressed. "Such a beautiful memory."

She paused while she envisioned Andrew's childhood memory, and then she added, "How great it would be if our children could have such a precious memory of us some day."

Andrew picked up the letter again and read on.....

> **All of our brothers and sisters were here for the funeral, even the ones in Christiania. We hope you had a good voyage. You seem so far away, but I hope we can keep in touch with you. The rest of the family sends greetings.**
>
> **John Adolph**

Many evenings Andrew got out his violin. Playing his violin was his release.

It would relax him, but it would also reveal his feelings. The tempo of the music would disclose whether he was worried or in good spirits.

One night, after listening to her husband play a sad melody, Inger asked him, "Is something troubling you, *Andreas*?"

"Well, I get so impatient. We have been here for almost six months now, and I tell myself, 'I didn't come to America to work in a bakery.'"

"You must give it time, *Andreas*. People will soon get to know you and your musical qualifications."

On November 9, 1889, Andrew and Inger's address was changed from *Dakota Territory, U.S.A*, to *South Dakota, U.S.A*. In November, *Dakota Territory* was divided into *North* and *South Dakota*, and these two states were admitted into the *Union* of the *United States*. As a result of this, all the people living in these two states at that time were accepted as United States citizens. This meant that Andreas (now with the American name of *Andrew*), Inger, Inez, Reinhart (now with the American name of Ray), *Andreas, Jr.* (now known as Andrew, Jr.) and Jennie all became United States citizens that day.

A band had been organized in Sioux Falls – the *Valhalla Band*. Andrew's friend, Carl Christiansen, had been taking cornet lessons from Andrew so he could join this band. When others discovered that Andrew was giving lessons, many came to him with their instruments. He now came to be known as *Professor* Indseth.

Some young people who wanted to learn to play the violin were glad to find a music teacher. Now life was good. Teaching music was what Andrew liked to do. He became so busy that he gave up his bakery job.

The new year of 1890 brought another child into the Indseth family. Berger was born March 10, 1890. When Ragna, Inger's friend, heard about the new arrival, she came over with a kettle of *rømmegraut* (cream porridge).

"It's a Norwegian custom," she said. "The new mother must have extra nourishment."

To help Inger, Ragna took little Jennie and Andrew, Jr. home with her for a few days. Ray, who wasn't quite six, went to play with the neighbor children. Inger needed her eight-year-old daughter, Inez, home from school to help her with the new baby.

When it came time for little Berger's baptism, Inger got out the long white baptismal dress and cap she had made for Jennie. "I'll need to get these washed," she decided. She also got out her *Nordmøre bunad* (costume). "I think I'll wear it to the baptism." She hadn't worn it during the last hot summer.

The white linen blouse with the long sleeves and large collar would need to be ironed, but Inger decided to try it on anyway. She then slipped into the long black woolen skirt, and tied the long black satin apron over it. Inger picked up the shiny gold colored brocade vest, which was the loveliest part of the costume. The design in the brocade was a soft gold, with the background a soft shade of red. She put it on.

To complete the costume was the wide red linen belt with embroidery stitches of gold, green and black. A matching cloth purse would hang at her side, and the little embroidered cap would be tied under her chin with a wide black bow.

While she had her costume on, Andrew walked in. "Oh, Inger, you look so nice...and so Norwegian!"

"Putting on this *bunad* makes me feel so dressed up and young again. And yes, it makes me feel Norwegian. I plan to wear it to Berger's baptism."

"You always looked so pretty in your *bunad*."

There was a decision that needed to be made. Andrew brought it up.

"I think we should ask Carl and Ragna Christiansen to be Berger's god parents. What do you think?"

"I agree, *Andreas*. That would be my choice too."

And so Berger was brought to church when he was six weeks old and his parents had him baptized, as they had their other children. They wanted their babies to be members of God's family.

* * * * *

About once every week or two, some of Andrew's men acquaintances in Sioux Falls would join him. He would get out his tuning fork and they would sing Norwegian songs together. Such great camaraderie! Being with other immigrants and speaking and singing in their native tongue brought a good feeling. You could take the men out of their native country, but you couldn't take away their love for the land of their birth, and its language and its music.

As time went by, there was more and more interest in starting a *Mandskor* (men's chorus) in Sioux Falls. Andrew noticed that there was a good balance of tenors, basses and baritones in the men who were interested. This would produce a good singing group, he thought. Andrew had obtained a catalog listing music from the Jensen Publishing Company in Chicago. This company published Norwegian material, song books, hymnals and sheet music. Andrew noticed two books – one, a collection of two, three, and four part songs for male chorus, and the other - a book of religious choral songs for male voices (*Religiose Korsanger for Mandsstemmer*). There was also an interesting book entitled Scandinavian Songs, which was a collection of national folk airs with both Norwegian and English texts and arranged for choruses. All of these books would be good for men's choruses, Andrew felt.

In December of 1890, Andrew was along with the group of interested men who organized the *Minnehaha Mandskor* in Sioux Falls. Because he had worked with men's choruses before, Andrew helped get the organization going.

The following year the *Minnehaha Mandskor* received information that an organization of Scandinavian men's choruses in the Midwest was being formed. The purpose of this organization was to cultivate an interest in Scandinavian songs. This meeting would take place in Minneapolis in September of 1891. The *Minnehaha Mandskor* sent Andrew to Minneapolis to represent them at this meeting and help with the organizing. The choruses in this organization were from Minneapolis, St. Paul, and Duluth, Minnesota; Sioux City and Fort Dodge, Iowa; Grand Forks, North Dakota; Omaha, Nebraska; and the Sioux Falls *Minnehaha Mandskor*.

At this meeting in September of 1891, the *Northwestern Scandinavian Singers Association of America* came into being. It was decided to have a *Sangerfest* (song festival) every other year, when all of the choruses would meet together. At these festivals, the individual groups would perform separately, and they would compete for prizes. But there also would be some numbers when all of the choruses would join together in song. *What powerful music that would be*! Andrew was excited to think about that.

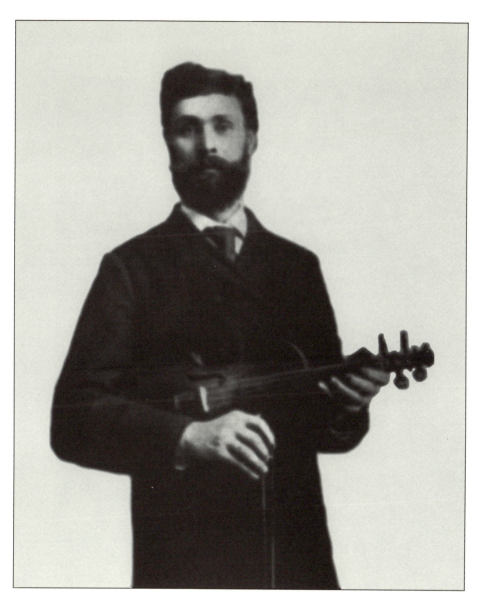

Andrew Kristian Indseth - 1903

Grieg Sangforening - 1894
Professor Indseth, 4th from right in front row, with baton.

Chapter 7

*I*n the school year of 1891-1892, Andrew and Inger had three of their children attending school in Sioux Falls: Inez, ten years, Ray, eight years, and Andrew, Jr., six years. Andrew was already giving Ray lessons on the clarinet.

Andrew and Inger were to add another member to their family on March 17, 1892, when Malinda was born. Now Inger was a very busy mother with four-year-old Jennie, and two-year-old Berger at home with her every day, and now the new baby! Inger for a short time kept Inez home to help her.

By the year 1893, Andrew was becoming very involved with his music. One afternoon he placed some song books, his tuning fork, and baton in a small suitcase and headed for the depot in Sioux Falls. He boarded the train departing southward. He hadn't been on the train very long when the conductor announced, *"Harrisburg"*, and several people got off. Through the train window, Andrew studied the Dakota scenery as the train passed the fields and farmsteads.

When the conductor called out *"Canton"*, Andrew picked up his suitcase and headed for the door. Canton was a town located twenty miles southeast of Sioux Falls. Tonight he was to meet with interested men singers from Canton who had contacted him. They wanted to form a men's chorus, and they had asked him to be their instructor and leader. Andrew's home was still in Sioux Falls, but with such good train connections, he had accepted the position. There was a late train to Sioux Falls that ran every night which he could take for his return trip.

Andrew had intentionally taken an early afternoon train today so he would have time to get acquainted with this town before the evening meeting and look for the hall where they would meet. Main Street, with all of its shops and stores, was only four blocks from the depot.

That evening twenty-one men gathered. They were all first or second generation Norwegian-Americans. The men introduced themselves to Andrew. There was John Anderson of the furniture store; John Isakson and E.S. Hanson, who each had dry goods and grocery stores; G. S. Hanson of the Eagle Drug Store; the Honorable Charles O. Knudson, Judge and lawyer; Register of Deeds L.T. Wirstad; Dr. Hendrickson; and E. O. Hofstad. Many of the others were businessmen, or else they worked in a business or office in Canton: T.H. Helgerson, A. Nelson, H. Anderson, William Nelson, L. H. Hanson, K.C. Berg, H. Greguson, J. E. Vichre, Otto Schmidt, T. Westby, Hans Graneng, H. F. Quien, and J. P. Nordseth. Several were farmers living north of Canton.

This meeting was for the purpose of getting the men's chorus organized. Andrew was anxious to hear their voices. He listened as he had them sing some simple songs to get an idea of how the voices sounded together. Andrew was pleased with the balance of tenors, baritones and basses, and he felt that there were great possibilities for this group.

The question came up as to what this group's name should be. Someone mentioned that the *Minnehaha Mandskor* used the name of their county – Minnehaha. Another man remarked that *Lincoln Mandskor* would sound so common. (Canton was located in Lincoln County.)

"We are a Norwegian organization and it should have a name that projects that fact."

One man suggested, "Why don't we name it after Norway's most famous musician – *Edvard Grieg*?"

When it went up for a vote, they finally decided to call themselves *The Grieg Sangforening* or *The Grieg Singing Society*. It was also voted to join the larger organization – *The Northwestern Scandinavian Singers Association of America*.

Professor Indseth informed them that the second *Sangerfest* of the new *Northwestern Scandinavian Singers Association of America* would be held in Sioux City. "In 1894, one year from now, the *Sangerfest* in Sioux City is what we should begin to prepare for."

The group of twenty-one men were very enthusiastic, and they all had the desire to make their organization an excellent one. Andrew soon had them working on a variety of selections, from Norwegian songs, to religious chorals.

Thus began Professor Indseth's weekly train trip from Sioux Falls to Canton for the regular Grieg chorus practice.

* * * * *

In the Midwest, the majority of Norwegian immigrants were living on farms, instead of in towns. One of the reasons for this was that the farms in Norway, back in the 1800's, had been small and the families were large, and there wasn't enough land for the boys who wanted to farm. When land opened up in the Midwest in America, it was *the land* that was the drawing card which brought many Norwegians to America and made farmers of them. This was especially true in the Canton area. It was *Norwegian* immigrants who were the pioneers that settled the land there in the late 1860's and early 1870's, both north and south of Canton. Now in the 1890's these communities were still solid Norwegian.

Ten miles south of Canton was a country store and church. This was the Moe community. It was located in the center of Norwegian farm homes which stretched more than five miles to the north, east, south and west of Moe.

The Moe community was a *little Norway* in itself. A ten mile ride to Canton with horse and buggy wasn't made very often because here they had a country store where Norwegian was spoken, and where the farmers could get their food and other supplies, even shoes and clothes. Here they could bring their eggs to trade for groceries, and sell their cream, and here they would gather to learn the news of the community.

On Sundays they would assemble at this church to listen to the sermon in Norwegian, meet their neighbors and visit with them in their native tongue.

There was a choir in the community, which included members of the Moe Church and the neighboring Trinity Church, and they called themselves the *Normanna* choir. They furnished music for church services and other community events, singing both Norwegian and English selections. Attending these choir practices was the social life of the young people.

Now a group of young farm men and newcomers in the Moe community was determined to have a brass band also, and perhaps even an orchestra. These were young farm men and boys who hadn't been trained in any instruments before.

Some of these young men didn't even have a complete grade school education. In pioneer days, if the sons were needed for farm work, especially at planting and harvest times, they had to miss school. The farm work came first. These were men who were up early every morning, working with hard physical labor all day long, and then before their day was ended, they had to take care of the livestock and milk the cows. *Yet they wanted to make music*, and having their own band was their dream.

When some of the young men of the Moe community heard of a Professor Indseth in Sioux Falls, who gave lessons and directed choirs and bands, they contacted him and persuaded him to come and help them. This would be a challenge for Andrew. Even getting to their practices would be a challenge and would be difficult for Andrew. After arriving in Canton by train, he would have to hire a horse and buggy from the Gate City Livery stable in Canton and drive the ten miles to Moe.

The Moe Band boys met for practice in a one room school house – the Rise School – which was one-half mile east of Moe. Saturday was their practice night. Professor Indseth made some simple musical arrangements for the group, and it didn't take long until they sounded like a band. By summer, outsiders were even welcomed to listen to them play.

* * * * *

In the spring of 1893, Andrew had taken on another project – a band in Canton, and this meant another practice night in Canton for Andrew. The city of Canton was located on the Sioux River, and an excursion steamboat had been built which ran on the Sioux River during the summer. Sometimes the Canton Band would have their practice outdoors on the deck of the "*City of Canton*" steamboat. The people living in the southern part of Canton by the river were delighted to sit on their lawns on a summer evening and listen to band music.

One hot August day, which was even hotter in Inger's kitchen in Sioux Falls because she was baking bread for her family, Andrew came in and sat down at the kitchen table. Then he shocked her with this statement, "I think we should move to Hudson."

Inger turned and stared at him. She looked puzzled.

"Both the children and I will hate to leave our friends here in Sioux Falls."

Andrew tried to explain, "All of these trips to Canton and Moe from Sioux Falls are just too much traveling. I figure if we moved to Hudson I could get my own horse and buggy and it would save so much time. Then I would only need to drive the nine miles from Hudson to the Moe Band practice. There are good train connections from Hudson which could take me to Canton for Grieg practice, and for the lessons I give there, and for the Canton Band practice. Also, Hudson is talking about starting a band. At least, to start with, there are a few who want lessons down there."

"Yes, *Andeas*, I agree that you spend too much time traveling. I can see your reasoning for moving to Hudson."

She sighed, and then added, "You'll have to do what is best. But if you decide to move, we should do it before the children start a new school year. And with another baby on the way, the sooner we can get the moving over with, the better it will be for me."

Andrew moved his family to Hudson, South Dakota, the first of September, 1893. The town of Hudson was located about twenty miles southeast of Canton. It was situated on the Sioux River also, and in the early days it had been a fording, or river crossing location.

Chapter 8

*A*ndrew came back from the General Store in Hudson, the town of his new residence. He set the heavy sack of flour down. His two oldest sons followed him, carrying in the rest of the groceries.

"I had a nice visit with the store proprietor, a Peter Overseth. He welcomed us to Hudson. Overseth has been here with his store almost since the town of Hudson was founded, when it was known as Eden. Someone told me that he has acted like a bank in Hudson. If someone needed to borrow money, they would go to him."

"What part of Norway is he from?" Inger asked.

"*Vestre Toten*," Andrew replied. "I discovered that he is interested in music. He was hoping we could get a band started here. The man said soon after he came, they had a cornet band. He was the leader. It seems he and several other men had been in town bands in Norway. However, now most of these men are gone."

One night, about two months after their move to Hudson, Inger awakened Andrew in the middle of the night.

"*Go and get the jordmor*! (midwife)."

Klara, the midwife, lived down the street from the Indseths.

"But, Inger, I thought it would be a month or two yet."

"Go, *Andreas*!"

A baby boy was born that night, but the midwife's report wasn't encouraging. "The baby is very weak, and tiny. I could hardly hear his birth-cry. I don't know what chance he has to live. I'm sorry."

Early the next morning, Inger sent Andrew to get the pastor to have the baby baptized. He was christened James. Andrew also had the town doctor come and check the baby. "He was just born too early," the doctor told them. "There is nothing you can do."

Several days after that, Andrew and Inger and their family stood on a hillside west of Hudson, in the Eden cemetery. The pastor had a graveside service for little James. As they stood around the grave, Inger suggested to her oldest daughter, Inez Amanda, "Do you suppose you children could sing that English song you learned in Sunday School?"

The children took hold of each other's hands. Inger studied her children as they stood in a semi-circle around the grave. There were the older ones – Inez Amanda, Ray and Andrew, Jr., and the younger ones – Jennie and Berger. Andrew held Malinda, the toddler, in his arms. Each one was so precious to her.

Her oldest daughter began singing........

> *Jesus loves me, this I know,*

Then the rest of the children joined their voices with hers.......

> *For the Bible tells me so.*
> *Little ones to Him belong,*
> *They are weak, but He is strong.*

The children knew the chorus so well that when they came to that part of the song, the singing became louder.

> *Yes, Jesus loves me,*
> *Yes, Jesus loves me,*
> *Yes, Jesus loves me,*
> *The Bible tells me so.*

Inger closed her eyes, and sent up a prayer, *"Thank you, God, for these six healthy and loving children you have given us....and also thank you for the two that are with You now, but whom I will see again some day."*

The November day that had been so cloudy and gray, now brightened as the sun broke through the clouds.

* * * * *

February 2, 1894, was an important date on Andrew's calendar. The Canton *Grieg Sangforening* was having their annual concert, which this year was to be composed of home talent. The Chorus had been working on their music. Andrew himself had spent a great deal of time with his violin because he was to play a violin solo at the concert, and a violin duet with Mr. Greguson, one of the members of the Grieg Chorus. Every morning now, the family had been listening to their father warm up his vocal chords by singing scale exercises in preparation for the vocal duet he would sing with another Grieg member.

One day Klara, their neighbor down the street, stopped to have a cup of coffee with Inger, and Inger was telling her about the concert.

"But I don't think I can go," Inger said. "I don't feel I can leave the children alone for that long. We would have to go by train in the afternoon and it would be late before we got home. Inez Amanda is almost twelve now, and she says she can take care of her brothers and sisters, but I don't feel right about it."

"*You must go to the concert, Inger!*" Klara insisted. "Don't worry about the children. I'll come over and everything will be taken care of. I want to do it. *You must go.*"

Inger enjoyed the Grieg concert very much. She was so proud of her husband. There had been so much applause, which told her that everyone else had enjoyed it also.

When the weekly newspaper from Canton came out the next week, it had a write-up about the event.

> The February 2nd concert given by the Grieg Sangforening last Tuesday night in Bedford Hall was a gratifying surprise to everyone present. All expected fine entertainment, but hardly anyone was prepared for the surprise, and the perfect success, from the opening address by John Isakson down to the last swing of Director Indseth's baton.
>
> It began with an instrumental number by Mollie Helgerson on the piano, which gave the young lady a fine opportunity to display her splendid training.
>
> Mr. Westby sang a comic song, with a guitar accompaniment.
>
> A violin overture by Professor Indseth, with an accompaniment by Miss Helgerson on the piano, was charming.
>
> The numbers by the Grieg Chorus were well received.
>
> "*The Silvery Sioux*", a composition by Palma Anderson, the twelve year old daughter of John Anderson, was played on the piano for the first time in public by the youthful composer.
>
> Gunda Jacobson, a school teacher in Canton, gave a presentation, mimicking a country school debating society.
>
> Next, was a violin duet by Indseth and Greguson, assisted by Miss Helgerson on the piano, and a vocal duet by Indseth and another Grieg member, Mr. Nelson.
>
> Then came the closing numbers by the twenty-one members.

As an ending to the musical evening, Director Indseth swung his golden baton and away went the voices in glorious harmony, strolling out in grand solo, duet, and chorus until with a flourish, the baton closed the melody of voice, and the audience loudly applauded.

The Hall was packed, with some people standing on the stairs.

* * * * *

When the 1893-94 school year in the Hudson School District was finished, the Indseth children were home, helping with the packing. *The Indseth's were moving to Canton*! Today some of the Moe Band boys were coming to help them get their possessions loaded and transported to their new home there.

Several of the band boys showed up early with their teams of horses and their lumber wagons with the high box sides. Other men came to help get the wagons loaded. Out came Inger's black kitchen stove, and the pot belly heating stove, and the large Norwegian trunk, and the beds and tables and dishes, and all the boxes of clothes and miscellaneous things.

"Don't forget my wash tub and scrub board," Inger reminded them.

The last things on the wagon were the kitchen chairs, which would ride on the top.

Another band member was going to take some of the family in his surrey. Andrew would drive his horse and one-seated buggy, and the two oldest boys would ride with him.

Inger took a last walk through the house to see if they had forgotten anything.

"We're ready to go," Andrew announced.

The procession, with Andrew in the lead, headed towards Canton. Sitting with him in his buggy were Ray and Andy, Jr..

Next, came the surrey with one of the band boys driving, and Inger and the rest of the children. In the back of the surrey was food and other household things.

Finally, following in the rear, was the chair-topped lumber wagon, and the other wagon with the rest of their possessions.

Andrew and Inger had talked it over, and they had agreed that they should make the move to Canton.

"This summer is going to be a busy time with many extra practices for the Grieg," Andrew told her.

The *Northwestern Scandinavian Singers Association of America* would be having their *Sangerfest* in Sioux City, and the Grieg boys would have to prepare for the singing competition.

"Anyway," Andrew said, "I think Canton is a more central spot to have our home. Often the Grieg Chorus is called upon to sing at different events, and with the Canton Band rehearsals there, and the private lessons I give in Canton, I'll not have to make so many train trips anymore."

Andrew had found a house with a small barn behind it where he could keep his horse. "There's room for another horse too," he said.

Inger suggested that they get a cow. "It is so hard to keep a supply of milk on hand for the children. If we had a cow, the boys would have some chores to do. That would be good for them."

Andrew had been spending a lot of time working on music with his sons. Ray had his clarinet, and Andrew had obtained a trombone for Andy. Their father would listen to them practice and give them pointers on how to do it right. He would join them with his cornet, and they would have a little band all by themselves. Andrew wanted his boys to enjoy music as much as he did. And they did! It is only natural that young sons would want to follow in their father's footsteps.

Andrew had purchased another instrument – this one for himself. He was now the owner of a piano, which was much needed for his work.

Inger opened the envelope they had received in the mail. She read......

> You are invited to the wedding of John Isakson and Jennie Mathison on Thursday, July 7, 1894, at 5 p.m. at the Bethlehem Lutheran Church in Canton, South Dakota.

Inger called Andrew, who was working on some music arrangements. "*Andreas*, one of your Grieg men is getting married and we are invited to the wedding."

Andrew knew all about it.

"John has asked the Grieg Chorus to present several numbers at the reception. You have to go too!" Andrew informed her. "The children will be alright. We'll only be a few blocks away, and if they need us they can soon find us. The members of the Chorus have already collected money for a gift. They plan to buy a silver tea set, which will be from all of the Grieg members and me."

July 7, 1894, turned out to be a lovely day. The wedding was performed at the Bethlehem Lutheran Church by Rev. O. E. Hofstad, with John Anderson at the organ. The reception was held at John Isaakson's residence, outside under the shade trees on the west side of the house, where a long table had been set up. Here the guests feasted, toasted, sang and made speeches. The *Grieg Sangforening* presented many numbers, and the voices of these singers were heard over half of the town. The festivities continued until an early hour, but Inger and Andrew left after the last Grieg Chorus number was finished. Inger was concerned about her children, who were home alone.

* * * * *

Now the time had come! Andrew and the Grieg Chorus had been practicing for it, and now it was time to perform at the great Scandinavian *Sangerfest* in Sioux City, Iowa. On July 12, 1894, the twenty-one members of the *Grieg Sangforening* left on the Tuesday train for Sioux City, and would not be home until Friday.

Many of the wives accompanied them. The women had been working on a beautiful banner, made of rich materials, with the name *Grieg Sangforening, Canton, South Dakota* embroidered on it. This would be used in the parade.

But Inger was not with them. "I can't leave the children alone for *four* days," she explained.

The Sioux Falls *Minnehaha Mandskor* was at the *Sangerfest* also, and Andrew enjoyed visiting with many of his old friends again. It was especially enjoyable to see Carl Christiansen again, who informed him that he and his wife, Ragna, planned to come to Canton to visit them soon.

At the first *Northwestern Scandinavian Singers Sangerfest* in Sioux Falls in 1892, the Sioux Falls wives of the *Minnehaha Mandskor* had made a beautiful and expensive banner with the words *Northwestern Scandinavian Singers of America* embroidered on it, and this was to be the trophy which the winner in the singers' competition at each *Sangerfest* would take home. Now at the Sioux City *Sangerfest*, the *Minnehaha Mandskor* had won the first prize and would take the banner home themselves, but to everyone's surprise, the second prize went to the youngest chorus, the new singing group from Canton, the *Grieg Sangforening*, under the direction of Professor A.K. Indseth. The Grieg group was also proud to receive first prize for the banner their wives had made for the parade. Andrew and all the members of the Grieg were very happy and satisfied. They felt their trip to Sioux City to their first *Sangerfest* competition had been a success.

The Grieg Chorus wanted to honor their wives for making the winning banner for the parade at the *Sangerfest*. To show them their appreciation, they invited them on Tuesday evening, August 2, to Mr. and Mrs. Gus Hanson's home for a very enjoyable lawn party. Inger accompanied Andrew. The Hanson lawn was one of the neatest in town and when it was lit up with Chinese lanterns and lamps, it had a bewitching effect. Fifteen young ladies, dressed in white, did the serving of ice cream and cake, and the men were furnished with cigars since it happened to be Mr. Hanson's thirty-fifth birthday. That night the Grieg men sang songs for their own enjoyment, but the sound of their music spread on the evening air to all the Canton neighborhood.

The first part of September, Carl and Ragna Christiansen came by train from Sioux Falls to visit their friends, Andrew and Inger, in their Canton home. Ragna and Inger hadn't seen each other since the Indseth's moved to Hudson, and they had much to share with one another.

The day they came, happened to be the night for Andrew to go to the band practice at Moe, and Carl rode along with him out there. They visited along the way. Carl was a member of the Valhalla Band in Sioux Falls and was interested in listening to Andrew's Moe Band boys.

The Christiansens stayed in Canton with Inger and Andrew overnight. Their visit was a fun time for the whole family. The Christiansens could see how the children had changed in one year.

Ragna picked up little Malinda, who now was two years old.

"You have grown to be such a big girl," Ragna told her.

She helped Inger dress the little girl and braid her hair that morning.

Carl put Berger, the four-year-old, on his lap. He felt especially close to him because he was his godparent. He wanted Berger to get to know him, but after a year, Berger was shy with him. Carl looked at Berger's new shoes, and remarked that he had "*big boy*" shoes now.

"*Nei, jeg har preste sko,*" (No, I have *preacher* shoes) he told Carl.

Andrew laughed, and said, "We have been teasing him about his new shoes."

"How about if I give you a horsey ride, Berger?" Carl asked.

Carl crossed his legs and placed Berger on his foot, and then he bounced him up and down. Carl remembered the little Norwegian ditty he used with his own children when they were small, which he began to chant as Berger rode on his foot.

	(translation)
Ride, Ride Ranke,	Ride, Ride the hobby horse.
Hesten heiter Blanke,	The pony's name is Blanke;
hesten heiter Apalgraa	It is a dapplegray.
Sit ei liti gjenta paa.	A little girl sits on it,
Salen var av silketoy	On a saddle of silken cloth.
Rid seg ned til Lisleby.,	She is riding down to Lisleby.

Det var ingen hjemme	But there was no one home
Men to smaa hunder,	But two small dogs,
Som sat bortved veggen,	That sat by the wall
Buste paa sitt skjegg,	Wiggling their whiskers,
Dille paa sin rumpe	And wagging their tails,
Og sa, "Voof, Voof, Voof!"	Saying, "Woof, Woof, Woof!"

"Do it *again*!" Berger called out as soon as Carl had finished. Andrew was standing and watching them.

"Are you having a good time, Berger?" he asked.

Berger didn't answer, because he was busy begging.... *"Do it again!"* *"More*!"

Carl smiled. He told Andrew, "I don't think there is a child in this world who doesn't enjoy *Ride, Ride, Ranke*.

Andrew wanted Carl to hear how well his two older boys were doing on their instruments, and Ray and Andy, Jr. each played short pieces for him.

The visit ended as Carl and Ragna boarded the train for Sioux Falls that evening, after spending almost two days with their friends, Inger and Andrew.

The Grieg Chorus ended the year of 1894 with a concert on December 21, in the Bedford Hall. Besides giving enjoyment to the audience, they realized thirty-seven dollars for the benefit of the Beloit Orphan's Home, located just southeast of Canton.

Chapter 9

*J*t was a very pleasant January day, and Andrew was happy for that. Tonight, January 14, 1896, the *Grieg Sangforening* was attempting something different. They had rented a suite of rooms in the Pattee block of downtown Canton. To initiate their new home, they had invited 150 of their friends to visit them and enjoy the evening listening to the excellent program they had prepared.

The Grieg men assembled early and did some warm-up exercises to clear their voices. Outside, the buggies began to pull up and deposit guests, and soon the hitching posts all around the block were taken. The men were happy to see such a good turn-out. Everyone was in a good mood and the guests were graciously welcomed.

This event was much more informal than a concert and was enjoyed by both the guests and their *Grieg Sangforening hosts*. Piano and vocal solos, duets, quartets, sextets, octets, and music by the entire Grieg Chorus were among the enjoyable features of the evening. Andrew had been busy locating music for all these various groups and working with them.

At the close of the musical numbers, remarks were made by President G. S. Hanson, and some of the other Grieg members, after which both guests and hosts sat together and visited at the nicely decorated tables as lunch was served. The consensus was that it was a delightful evening, and the Grieg boys felt it was a success.

January had already been a busy month for Andrew. Before the *Grieg Sangforening* event, his Canton Band had had a concert on January 10, which had band music interspersed with local vocal and instrumental musical numbers. The purpose of this concert was to assist the band financially so the present bandmaster (who was Professor Indseth) could be retained. Andrew made his living from salaries from the various musical organizations he instructed and directed, besides the private lessons he gave. From time to time, the organizations had concerts to raise that money.

The Bedford Hall, which was where concerts were usually held in Canton, had been deteriorating and now it was being renovated and redecorated. The stage was being rebuilt and all the inside was being painted. New dressing rooms were being constructed, and the scenery was being repaired and cleaned. At one point, the question had been, "Shall we repair and remodel it, or should it be torn down and a new building erected?" The first option was decided upon.

It was because of this renovation at Bedford Hall that the Grieg boys had rented these other facilities for their annual winter concert, and now they enjoyed having their weekly practices in those rooms.

Andrew sat in his chair, reading the *Canton Farmers Leader*. He had taken time out from his music to catch up on the Canton news. An article about the college caught his eye. All of a sudden Andrew began laughing.

Inger looked over at him with a puzzled expression on her face. She was feeding six-month old Josephine, who had been born last August 15, in 1895. Josephine was Andrew and Inger's seventh child.

"What's so funny, *Andreas*?" she asked.

"Inger, you have to hear this!"

Andrew read the article from the February 5, 1896, newspaper –

> Study was considerably interrupted Tuesday at Augustana College. A Notary Public was busy taking affidavits of gentlemen students who all swore they had nothing to do with the pig found in the ladies hall about 10 pm Monday. The poor pig's feet were tied together, but to the credit of the little porker, it may be said he never squealed on the boys who perpetrated the joke.

"Those college boys!" Andrew exclaimed. "But it was so funny! Just think of what excitement there must have been in the ladies hall! And the editor wrote it up so cleverly! Boys will be boys!"

The Augustana College, which had been moved from Wisconsin to Beloit, and then to Canton, was finding it difficult to get established because of the hard economic times, and other problems, but President Tuve deserved praise for the determined effort he was making to keep the school going. Finally, in the fall of 1895, when the new school year began, there were an increased number of students and the whole Canton community was happy to see the school going forward. The newspaper tried to keep the readers informed of the activities there.

About three miles east of Canton, on the other side of the Sioux River, was the state of Iowa. To cross the river, there was a location where the river could be forded. Continuing on about five miles east would bring you to the town of Inwood, Iowa. Andrew had been instructing and directing an orchestra there, and also a band.

Andrew had been making weekly trips into Inwood for the orchestra and band practices, always using the fording location. The only bridge across the Sioux was a number of miles south of there at Beloit, which wasn't convenient. One night, while Andrew was directing at a concert in Inwood, there had been a rainstorm. On the way home, when he got to the crossing spot, the river was too high to ford. Andrew wondered whatever could he do? He had on his good black conductor's suit, with the lapels of black satin, and he had his precious violin along. He didn't want either one of these to get wet.

"All right!" he told himself, "I'll just have to put my violin on top of the buggy, take off my shoes and suit and put them up there too, and the horse and I will swim across!"

Inger was surprised when Andrew came home that night, dripping wet in his long underwear, but his special black suit was dry, and his violin was in fine shape. When a person had to do so much traveling with horse and buggy, he never knew what kind of weather he would come up against.

* * * * *

"*Andreas*, you received some mail from Norway today," Inger said, as she handed him the envelope. When he saw the return address – *Alexander Bull, Bergen, Norway* –he quickly opened and read it.

Dear Andreas,

When I was in Christiania last week attending a concert, I met your brother Hans. He gave me your United States address.

This summer I will be making a concert tour in the United States, playing my father's violin. I will be stopping in Minneapolis. On May 17 there will be the unveiling of a plaster cast of a statue of my father which will later be erected in Loring Park in Minneapolis. I have been asked to attend. I will be giving a concert there also.

Many times you have invited me to stop and see you. This time I will have a few extra days in my schedule, and these come

at a time when a few days of rest would fit in very well. It is about half way through my tour. If it is convenient for you and your wife, I would like to stop in Canton for a few days after my Minneapolis concert. About half way through my tour I usually need a little break. I must admit that I am not as young as I used to be.

Let me know if this will work for you. It will be good to visit with you again.

Alexander Bull

"Inger, we're going to have company from Norway!" Andrew paused a few moments and then he explained, "Ole Bull's son will stop in Canton to visit us. What a wonderful surprise! Now I'll get to learn all the latest news from the Norwegian music world."

Inger hadn't heard her husband this excited for a long time. Then she stopped to think what this would mean for her, and she became excited too. Her mind began planning. She'd have to do a thorough house cleaning and do some baking. Inger had never entertained anyone this important before.

"We'll have to fix up Inez and Jennie's bedroom for him," Inger said. "They can sleep in the little girl's bedroom. The little ones can sleep on the floor."

Andrew tried to calm her down by stating, "It will be almost two months before Alexander comes. His concert in Minneapolis isn't until May seventeenth. You'll have plenty of time to get ready."

Syttende Mai (May 17) was the Norwegian Independence Day, and Norwegian-Americans liked to celebrate that day. On May 17, 1896, the Norwegian community from the Centennial Church northwest of Inwood was acknowledging the date and had invited the Grieg Chorus of Canton to participate in the program. The Grieg boys presented a selection of Norwegian numbers. Members from this church and community had immigrated from Vest Agder, in southern Norway.

A couple of days later, at noon on the nineteenth of May, Andrew was at the Canton depot to pick up his friend from Norway. Alexander Bull got off the train, carrying the case with the precious *Guarnerius* violin of his father, Ole Bull.

Inger had a good meal waiting for them when they reached the house, and after eating, Inger suggested that Alexander go to the bedroom and *hvile* (rest), which he did. Later when he came downstairs, Andrew and his guest spent some time in the music room – two men and their violins.

Alexander Bull always put in some practice time every day. After he had finished, he asked Andrew if he would like to play his father's violin. It was a fantastic moment when Andrew was able to hold that *Guarnerius* violin in his hands, and it even felt better when he was allowed to play it. He began the tune of Ole Bull's composition "*Saeterjenten's Sondag*". This was a musical summit for Andrew – he was connecting with the famous violinist, Ole Bull, through his prized instrument and his famous composition.

"Tell me about the event in Minneapolis." Andrew was interested. "Did you have a good crowd at your concert? And tell me about the statue of your father."

"*Ja*, it was a big event! There were over six thousand people who turned out for the unveiling of the statue. However, it was a little sad, though, because Jacob Fjelde, the sculptor, after only finishing the plaster cast, passed away in February from an ear infection. But they will go ahead and have it cast in bronze, and a year from now that statue will be erected in Loring Park. It will be a handsome statue."

"What about your concert?"

"It was a full house. It was very meaningful for me because I was re-minded that my father had played concerts in that building two or three times in the past."

"I'm sure you still miss your father."

"Now it's been almost sixteen years since he died."

Alexander was quiet for a few moments. Then he continued...

"I will always remember the tribute that Edvard Grieg gave father the day of the funeral. They read it at the statue unveiling the other day. Here, I have a copy of it. You can read it"

> "Because you (Ole Bull) were above all others an honor to your country; because you above all others have raised our people to the sunlit heights of art; because you were the first pioneer of our new, more national music, above all others faithful, warm-hearted and soul-conquering; because you have thus planted a seed that will bear rich fruit in the future and for which coming generations will bless you; with a thousand and again a thousand thanks for all of this, I place this laurel wreath on your grave in behalf of Norwegian music. May you rest in peace."

Alexander again went on, "Did you know that I spent most of 1889 in Paris with Grieg? I organized the Paris concerts for him. Our families have always been close. It was my father that encouraged Grieg as a young boy to get musical training."

"You have been blessed by having so many fine musicians and such outstanding music in your life," Andrew told him.

The following day Alexander had opportunity to get a good rest, and the two men visited and had much conversation. They also played duets on the violins. Inger was a very gracious hostess, preparing tasty meals, but mainly, she let Alexander Bull get the rest he needed.

By the beginning of summer, the Bedford Hall was remodeled, redecorated and ready for use..... and the *Grieg Sangforening* was ready for a concert. On Friday, May 29, 1896, the Grieg Chorus entertained a Canton audience in the refurbished Bedford Hall. The *Canton Farmer's Leader* gave this report of the concert.

> The Grieg Sangforening delighted a Canton audience last Friday night with a delightful concert. The program was a good one and each part was rendered with artistic effect. Professor Indseth, as leader, deserves credit for his excellent management.
>
> Miss Mollie Helgerson, with the piano, proved to be all for which her most ardent admirers hoped. She is graceful and artistic in her work, and proved, as Augustana College Professor Petzel said, to be one of the few ladies in the Northwest who is competent to play Grieg masterpieces.
>
> Miss Palma Anderson, as a piano student, won much praise for her excellent work and she deserves it all. The little lady proved that with time and study she will be a master in this line.
>
> G. S. Hanson, Hans Anderson, H. Greguson, and another gentleman sang solos and duets, and merited the applause given them.
>
> Professor Indseth and Miss Louise Johnson, in a violin duet, were very good, and Miss Johnson was especially admired for her able execution.
>
> A cornet duet by Professor Indseth and Albert Oehmen was a special and pleasing feature.
>
> Professor Petzel's review of German and Scandinavian music, was a music gem in prose, and did honor to woman and music, both of which this Professor loves. It was a scholarly tribute to the elements that soften and refine the world, and no man in this country is better able to carry the banner of love and music than he.
>
> Besides numbers by the Grieg Chorus, the Inwood Orchestra was an important feature of the entertainment. The program was some of the best entertainment ever given in Canton.
>
> The Grieg Society is making Canton a music-loving community.

1896 was the year for the biennial *Sangerfest* of the *Northwestern Scandinavian Singers of America*. The organization met in July. The *Minnehaha Mandskor* of Sioux Falls had won first prize at the singing competition again.

That year there had been some dissatisfaction and dissension about the music competition. At the meeting, one man stood up and said, "We think we should come to the *Sangerfest* to enjoy each other's music instead of trying to outdo each other, and criticize each other."

Andrew agreed. "I'm sure each Chorus would still do their best, even if there weren't prizes."

It was decided to discontinue the competition and the prizes, and just sing for the enjoyment of singing. The Sioux Falls chorus had furnished the trophy banner that was the reward for being first place in these competitions, and besides, they had won it for two consecutive years, so it was decided that the *Minnehaha Mandskor* should take the banner home with them and keep it. And that settled the problem.

Later that summer, sadness came to the *Grieg Sangforening*. The wife of one of their members died. Just two years earlier, they all had attended John and Jennie Isakson's wedding, and celebrated and feasted with them that night, and had sung the night away as they gathered on the newlywed's lawn. Mrs. Isakson hadn't been well for over a year, and during the last week, her condition became critical. At her funeral, the Grieg Chorus sang *Den Store Hvide Flok* (Behold the Host Arrayed in White). As Andrew directed them, the sound of the men's voices, with all the parts blending, gave a glorious message on that sad day, and Andrew was pleased because music can bring to this world both enjoyment and soothing comfort.

Andrew was back out in the Moe community again. He had been contacted to direct the *Normanna Choir* there. Jens Bjorlie, who had been the director for many years, had returned to Norway in August, and on October 20, the group reorganized with a large membership, having Professor Indseth as their instructor.

1896 was a Presidential election year and a new man from Nebraska, William Jennings Bryan, was running for President. As his main running point, he was advocating *Free Silver*, and going off the gold standard. Everyone was talking and arguing politics. Many Lincoln County people believed in Bryan and his ideas.

He was campaigning, and on October 8, he came to South Dakota, leaving Sioux City by train. Many people waited to see him at the Hudson depot, but there the train only slowed down, while he stood in the rear of the train saluting and bowing. When the train got to Canton, a mob of people were waiting at the depot to see the candidate. He spoke for five minutes, and then went on to Sioux Falls. He was running against McKinley, but at the November election, it was McKinley who won the Presidency.

Another candidate in the 1896 election was Peter Overseth, the storekeeper from Hudson. He was running for state senator. When the ballots were counted in November, he also won. He would go to Pierre when the new South Dakota legislature session began the first of 1897.

* * * * *

On December 15, 1896, Andrew and Inger's eighth child was born. The baby was named Florence. There were only sixteen months between Josephine, who was born August 15, 1895, and the new baby Florence. The problem was that the new baby's birth was so close to Christmas.

"Aren't we going to have Christmas this year?" six-year-old Berger asked his father.

"What makes you say that, Berger?"

"Mama is so busy with the baby, she won't have time to make Christmas for us!"

"Oh, no, that isn't true. Of course, we will have Christmas. In fact, this Christmas will be the best Christmas we've ever had. This year we'll have a baby, just like they had at the first Christmas.

"No, Berger," Andrew further explained. "This year we are *all* going to help make Christmas! Ray, Andy, Jr. and I will go downtown and get what we need from the stores. I know we must get some *lutefisk* and a Christmas tree."

Then he informed his two oldest daughters, Inez, and Jennie, that he and they would do the baking. "You know I worked in a bakery for many years," he told them. "We must make *lefse* and some Christmas cookies. If I could fry doughnuts, I guess I can fry *fattigmand*!"

"The girls and I will take care of it, Inger. Don't worry. You just get rested up and take care of the baby now, so you'll be able to make supper on *Julekveld*. (Christmas Eve)"

It was a busy week, with baking, and cleaning. Everyone had jobs to do. On the day before Christmas, the tree went up and young and old helped decorate it.

There was one more task that had to be taken care of. Who was going to wash the kitchen floor? It was a Norwegian custom that before Christmas arrived, the house had to be sparkling clean for that holy time. The last cleaning job was the kitchen floor.

Andy, Jr. spoke up, "We have a mop, don't we?" "Yes," they told him. "Then I'll do it!" he volunteered. And he did.

While Inger and the girls were busy in the kitchen, preparing the usual Christmas Eve meal, with *lutefisk* and *lefse*, boiled potatoes, and all the trimmings, Andrew took over the job of tending the babies – both ten-day-old Florence and sixteen-month-old Josephine. Berger and Malinda gathered around him also. When the baby was asleep, Andrew put her in the cradle and held Josephine on his lap.

This was one of the shortest days of the year, and darkness settled early. Andrew told Berger and Malinda to go over to the window and see if they could see the star - the *Julestjerne* (Christmas star).

Berger put his nose against the windowpane.

"I can see some stars," he said.

Andrew went over to look.

"Berger, do you see that *bright* one?"

Both Berger and Malinda studied the night sky.

Andrew told them, "Perhaps that is the star that guided the three wise men so long ago."

"Ja, *Pappa*," agreed Berger. "I think that is the *Julestjerne*."

After the Christmas Eve supper, the family had their special musical Christmas program. The boys played Christmas songs on their instruments, and there was a lot of singing. Andrew had been teaching his sons to play many different instruments. Now both Ray and Andy, Jr., were learning to play the violin. Andrew had made some arrangements of the old Christmas carols for them, and everyone joined in singing the familiar ones.

The Christmas Gospel was read.

Andrew then picked up his violin and played some beautiful variations of *Glade Jul* (Silent Night), and other Christmas songs. As he stood there with his violin and played, it was almost as if he and the violin were one. The melody that came out of his instrument was his intense and sometimes contemplative feelings being displayed.

Jeg er saa Glad Vaer Julekveld (I am so glad each Christmas Eve) was the family favorite. Andrew said, "Now let's sing it!" Andrew accompanied them on the piano while everyone sang their hearts out.

They finished with *Glade Jul* (Silent Night). Their musical father had the family sing it *a cappella*. He directed them, sometimes having them sing softly, and sometimes bringing out certain parts, and it was pleasing to Andrew's ears. Every member of the family felt this was a holy night. After the program was finished, there were packages for everyone to open. About this time, the younger children were getting tired.

"Time for bed!" Andrew announced.

Andrew took six-year-old Berger and four-year-old Malinda upstairs and put them to bed. When he said good-night to Berger, the little fellow put his arms around his father's neck, and said, "*It was a good Christmas, Pappa!*"

EPWORTH LEAGUE ASSEMBLY HALL, CANTON, S. D.

Chautauqua Auditorium, Canton, South Dakota - Circa 1902

Chapter 10

$\int$he members of the *Grieg Sangforening* didn't only have concerts and weekly practices. In the summer of 1898, they planned an outing to Spirit Lake, a resort community in Iowa. Their families – their wives and children – were included. The train from Canton was running special excursion rates to Spirit Lake at only $1.50 a round trip, for adults.

"Does everyone have their swimming suits and towels?" Andrew was checking on his family.

"And Ray, you carry the lunch basket."

Inger had filled the basket with sandwiches, and doughnuts and fruit. She had included some crackers for the toddlers to lunch on.

This would be something different for the Indseth family. The children were very excited. Inger had two little ones to care for, but she looked forward to being a part of the group of Andrew's musical friends and their families. It was a supreme event for the Indseth teenagers – fourteen-year-old Ray, twelve-year-old Andy, Jr., Inez, who was sixteen, and ten-year-old Jennie. There would be bathing and boating, all of which were a young person's idea of a good time. This also included a train ride, which was something they had not done often.

On the train ride back to Canton that evening, everyone was tired, and some of them were a little sunburned, but all had had a great summer experience.

The next year, on March 11, 1899, another son arrived in the Indseth family, another boy for Andrew to train for his family band. Now Inger and Andrew's family consisted of four sons, and five daughters, ranging in ages from seventeen years to the new baby, Roy Selmer. Inger's older girls were a big help to her now. Inez was able to bake delicious graham bread almost as tasty as her mother's.

For the next several years, the town of Canton went through a building boom. With work on the Federal Indian Asylum buildings, which would be constructed a mile east of Canton, work on a new Augustana College building, and work on the Chautauqua auditorium, new business houses and a number of fine large homes to be erected, Canton was a lively place.

In the fall of 1900, the Canton Public School system had two new school buildings ready for students, one on the west side of town, which some of the younger Indseth children attended, and one on the east side. Professor C. G. Lawrence, who had come to teach at the College, was now Superintendent of the Canton Public Schools. He had married the school teacher, Gunda Jacobson, and on August 1, 1900, a son whom they named Ernest O., was born to them.

People were very excited about something entirely new coming to Canton. The Epworth League of the Methodist Sioux Falls District was planning a Chautauqua in Canton. The town had donated fourteen acres, a most attractive site, plentifully wooded and lying on one of the prettiest parts of the Sioux River. The grounds were very accessible, only four blocks from the Milwaukee depot. The river was navigable for ten miles up to this point, so there was a splendid opportunity for boating and bathing. Bathing houses were being erected for both sexes.

Andrew was excited about having a Chautauqua in Canton, because it would bring the finest musicians and lecturers from the Midwest for their programs.

By the summer of 1901, several buildings had been built, among them a large auditorium, 146 feet by 124 feet, with the capacity for seating about three thousand persons, and with extra space for more. Up to five thousand could be protected from rain and sun under its roof. A dining hall, 32 feet by 70 feet, would be added, and several boarding houses, including a children's house, where children could play and be cared for. There would be room for hundreds of tents on the grounds, and some families were building cottages.

One of the attractive features was a new steamboat, *The Sioux Queen*, which would hold 200 people. Captain Hanson would have all he could do to accommodate all the people who would seek this pleasant and healthful recreation. A good supply of row boats would also be available.

Every year, for ten days around the Fourth of July, this spot in Canton would be like a fine resort with planned programs and activities by the Epworth League, bringing in prominent speakers and music from near and far. The facilities would be available for other events the rest of the year.

The businesses in Canton were progressing also. The P. S. Puckett Brothers' big double store would be the finest store in town when the papering and painting were finished. Everything was fixed in the latest style, in keeping with the elegant stock they handled. They had stylish women's suits, and the latest fashions in ladies clothes, children's clothes, curtains, rugs, calico and print cloth, sewing supplies, and miscellaneous necessary personal and household goods. The store was being wired for electric lights, which would be a great improvement.

Dr. Noid was adding new beautiful marble-based plate glass showcases and counters, and an elegant large soda fountain to his pharmacy. Soon long lines would be forming to buy his ice cream cones.

The Corner Drug Store had a soda fountain also. The store advertised that the gentle "sizz" of its lively soda fountain was a musical sound to those who enjoyed the delicious drinks served there.

The firm of Tossini Confectionery had begun to manufacture ice cream. They had installed a large refrigeration plant, and ordered a gas engine. This would enable them to make and serve the very best ice cream. Over the Fourth of July, in 1902, Tossini had so many ice cream orders that he had four men out hunting cream from farmers to fill his ice cream orders, and still by 6 p.m. on July 4, he was 250 gallons short.

Miss Helga Hage had the annual Spring Grand Opening of her millinery shop on May 2, 1901. It was the finest display of millinery ever seen in Canton. She had been to Minneapolis to buy her merchandise. Besides viewing the latest styles in hats, callers were treated to free coffee.

The Laxson Brothers advertised men's clothing and North Star fur coats.

A new bank was organized and opened in Canton on October 1, 1901. It was named the Farmers State Bank, with Peter Overseth, the Hudson storekeeper and state senator, as the president.

Hanson and Grevlos had a full line of groceries, with Rio coffee at 25 cents a pound, 10 lbs. of oatmeal for 25 cents, and 7 bars of soap for 25 cents, and they specialized in different kinds of Norwegian delicacies, fish, cheese, dried mutton, and so forth.

The Van Houten restaurant had the best twenty-five cent meals in the city.

The Gate City Bakery's raised doughnuts were available three times a week.

In 1901 the Chautauqua ran from July third to the fourteenth, with the best lecturers and educators in the country, and an array of talent that was sure to attract. On Sunday, all the Canton churches were closed so members could attend the Sunday service at the Chautauqua. On Monday evening, Miss Katharine Gemmill from Canton, with her lovely voice, performed. Tuesday was Veteran's Day, with veterans from the Civil War and the Spanish War. The first year of the Chautauqua turned out to be a grand success.

Canton was going to have a fine new hotel. After months of consideration and planning, insurance man, O. A. Rudolph, finally decided to erect a modern hotel at the corner of Fifth Street and Lincoln. Work began in September of 1901, with plans for completion in a year, at an estimated cost of $20,000.

The *Grieg Sangforening* had a busy year also, with a concert on April 24, 1901. Some of the highlights of the program were a duet by member G. S. Hanson and his wife, and a piano solo by Lajla Skartvedt.

No one doubted the ability of Grieg member, Hans Anderson, to sing a solo since the time long ago when he sang *"Mahoney's Fourth of July"*, and he was just as good that night. He was encored, but he just bowed and smiled.

The Grieg Chorus sang *"Festival March"*, followed by *"Landkjenning"*, which was accompanied by an orchestra. Mr. Sorum sang *"Saeterjentens Sondag"*, with the quintet accompanying him.

A guest, Katharine Gemmill, who had been studying music at a college in Yankton, sang Gounod's *"Kavatina"*, and her singing of the bravuras in *"The Nymph on the Rhine"* showed the control she had over her voice and her ability to execute rapid and difficult passages. To an encore, Miss Gemmill responded with a song in the Swedish language, which pleased the audience greatly.

Another Grieg member, Judge Charles Knudson, sang *"Bedouin Love Song"*.

The quintet that sang *"Asleep in the Deep"* made a hit with the audience.

Gus Engebretson sang a bass solo.

After a short curtain speech by Mr. Knudson, the program closed with a song by the Grieg Chorus entitled *"Good Night"*.

Mrs. Charles O. Knudson and Miss Lajla Skartvedt, as accompanists, and Professor Indseth, as director, deserve credit. The house was crowded.

On June 21, 1901, the Grieg Chorus sang several numbers at the 1901 Canton High School graduation. They rendered *"Home Sweet Home"* in such a manner as to receive a vigorous encore to which they responded with *"Saet Maskinen Igang"*. Miss Katharine Gemmill also sang. The graduating class's motto was *"Here Endeth the First Lesson."*

* * * * *

In June, a group of sixteen members of the Koshkonang, Wisconsin, branch of the Norwegian Pioneer Association of America came to Canton on an excursion. They were met at the train by the members of the *Grieg Sangforening*, along with a large group of old settlers and leading Norwegians from around the city. After listening to some singing by the Grieg, they were escorted to the new dining hall at the Chautauqua grounds, where they had dinner. After a smoker, they took a boat ride on the *Sioux Queen*, and on board listened to more songs by the Grieg Chorus and speeches by several other Norwegian Cantonites.

On June 20, 1901, the annual *Old Settlers Picnic* was held in Hudson. A large tent was set up, with banners and bunting. Professor Indseth's Canton Band opened the afternoon program and presented several numbers. There were speeches, and each of the old settlers was encouraged to relate briefly his or her experiences from pioneer days.

* * * * *

Friday, September 13, 1901 was a sad day for the United States. President McKinley had been shot. He died the next day. McKinley had won reelection in November, 1900. On Saturday, September 14, at 3:30 p.m., Vice President Theodore Roosevelt was sworn in as the new United Sates President. The whole country was shocked and in mourning.

McKinley's favorite hymn, "*Lead Kindly Light*", and his dying hymn, "*Nearer My God To Thee*", were played throughout the nation all of the next week.

* * * * *

"Is everyone ready?" Andrew called.

"For once, Inger, you won't have to make a meal for us," Andrew told her.

The Canton Lutheran Ladies Aid was holding a day-long festival and sale to raise money for Augustana College and missionary work, and they were serving a *lutefisk* meal.

"It's good for us to patronize the ladies of the church, and besides, everyone in our family enjoys *lutefisk*"

Andrew and his family went for the dinner, which was served from noon to 4 p.m. Supper was served from 4 p.m. until 7 p.m., and the sale of useful and fancy things was held in the evening. The women raised almost $200. $100 had been pledged toward furnishings for the college.

Rudolph Hotel - 1910
Canton, South Dakota

Chapter 11

*P*rofessor Indseth was always busy with private music lessons. He gave vocal instruction, and instruction on the violin, piano, cornet and other band instruments. At this time, neither the Canton High School, nor the Augustana College had bands, nor did they have band instructors.

Two of the students Andrew had were the Overseth boys, from the Moe community. They were the nephews of Senator Peter Overseth, now the president of the new Farmers State Bank in Canton. Both boys were attending Augustana College.

Martin had begun lessons on the cornet from Professor Indseth back when the Indseths lived in Hudson. Martin loved music, and now he desired to improve his cornet playing. His brother Anton, known as Tony, who was a few years younger, was beginning lessons on the trombone. Often when they were having their lessons, Andrew's two sons, Ray and Andy, Jr., sat in with them and they all played together. This was exciting and made Martin and Tony even more enthusiastic about their instruments.

Andrew always kept working with his sons. He had them trained both on cornet and violin, and Ray played the clarinet and Andy played the trombone. Professor Indseth felt that his sons were good enough now to take part in a concert. The Moe community in 1902 wanted to celebrate Norway's holiday on May 17, and they came to Andrew for suggestions for a program. He mentioned to them that he thought his family could present a concert. They had faith in Professor Indseth and were looking forward to what he would produce. The owners of the Moe Store had built a public hall next to the store, and this is where they would perform.

Andrew worked up a program which included a cornet trio with himself and his sons, violin duets by his sons, and clarinet and trombone solos. He himself played one of Grieg's compositions on the piano, as well as a violin number. Andrew decided the women in the family should take part also. Inger had a lovely coloratura soprano voice, and she sang "*Saeterjenten's Sondag*", while he accompanied her on the violin.

Andrew worked with Inez and Jennie on a fun Norwegian song "*Hvor mange penger hadde han?*" The audience really enjoyed that. It was about a mother who tells her daughter which suitor she can invite into the house. She always asked the key question... "*Hvor mange penger hadde han?*" (How much money does he have?) Andrew gathered the younger children up on the stage and they sang "*Per Spelmann*", while he played his violin, acting out the part of *Per Spelmann*, the fiddler.

The long hall was packed, and with the many opened windows on each side, people stood outside and listened also. The Indseth family received many encores, and they brought enjoyment to the crowd.

The first week in March, Andrew made a trip downtown, and came back with three cigars. He was quick to give Inger the news about his Grieg boys: Charles Knudson had become the father of a baby daughter on Monday, Ed Graneng had a baby girl on Tuesday, and Chris Berg, a few days later was also rejoicing over the arrival of a daughter. All three were handing out cigars that day.

"Well," Andrew said, "there won't be any future members for our *Grieg Sangforening* there!"

Palma Anderson, the young lady from Canton, was studying music in Chicago, and the Chicago *Skandinavian* newspaper paid her a compliment in an article about her recital.

> Miss Palma Anderson, a young and promising artist from Canton achieved extraordinary success in her recital January 17, at Ferry Hall Chapel. Miss Anderson rendered difficult selections, such as Concerto by Grieg, op 16, two numbers by Shumann, one Sonata by Beethoven, and two Etudes and one Prelude by Chopin.

* * * * *

On June 25, 1902, the annual Old Settlers' Picnic was scheduled to be held at the Chautauqua grounds. There were big plans for it. The people were to meet at Fifth Street and parade down to the auditorium, but late in the afternoon the weather became threatening and many left for home. South of Canton, in the Moe community, the weather produced a tornado. It followed a path westward from the Iowa border and at first destroyed the Trinity Church two miles east of Moe. It took the steeple off the new Lands Church at Moe, and then moving west three miles, destroyed the Romsdal Church. Along the way, most farms received damage to their buildings, but only one person living by the Iowa border was killed. For weeks afterwards, the lumber yard in Hudson was swamped with lumber wagons loading up lumber to repair the farms.

There hadn't been much damage as far north as Canton, so the Chautauqua, which ran from June 26 until July 6, went ahead as planned.

On July 11, the cornerstone was laid for the new Augustana College Main building. The President of the United Lutheran Synod delivered an address in Norwegian, and the Gate City band, the *Grieg Sangforening* and the Canton Lutheran Church choir furnished music. The plans were that the building would be finished in a year. President Tuve made the Board of Trustees a promise, *"I will fill every building you erect."* He still was working hard to make the college go forward.

1902 was again a year for the *Northwestern Norwegian Singers Association of America's* biennial *Sangerfest*. The event was to be held in Sioux Falls again on July 10, 11, and 12. The Canton Grieg members made arrangements with the railroad for a special car which would go up in the morning each day and return after the evening program so the Canton people could be home every evening. This car would be tastefully decorated and would not only advertise Canton and the singers, but it would be a convenience for others who attended.

The Grieg boys made a fine showing. They were given the post of honor in the parade, and accorded the privilege of being first in the chorus program. Also, in the selection of the *Sangerfest* director that year, Professor Indseth had many pulling for him, but he just missed the honor by several votes.

Later that summer, Andrew received a letter from his younger brother, John August, in Norway.

Dear brother,

Joachim and I have been considering a trip to America. As you have heard, Joachim has been working as a musician in Christiania. He plays the cornet, violin and piano. I've been playing the bass fiddle.

So far, I'm still single, but Joachim has been married again, as you know, and they have three children. He hopes his family will follow later, but Sofie doesn't sound very interested.

Would there be any opportunities for us in South Dakota? Let us know so we can go ahead with our plans.

John August

"Inger!" Andrew called. He read John August's letter to her. "What do you think of that?"

He didn't wait for her answer. "I'll have to write him and tell them they can stay with us until they find something different. You know, I could use them in some of my music groups. Dr. Wendt has been starting this orchestra that I am directing, and we're looking for violin players and a bass fiddler. And some of my bands could use Joachim's cornet. John August has an excellent bass voice that we could use for special numbers at our band concerts."

Then Andrew added, "But I don't know about Joachim leaving his family behind. We never did meet Sofie. There must be more to this than we know."

Inger agreed with him; "It was so sad when Petra, his first wife, died in 1891. I understood that it was very hard on Joachim."

Inger then gave Andrew her answer, "Yes, they can stay with us for a while. Just write and tell them."

* * * * *

The two Lutheran churches in Canton had belonged to different synods – one the Augustana synod and the other, the Norwegian synod. Now the two synods had merged and become the United Lutheran Church, so they didn't need two separate congregations in Canton any more. With two church buildings, it was difficult to know what to do. Neither one was very large. It was decided to put the two churches side by side. They moved the church from Second Street alongside the church on Third Street, and took out the joining walls, opening it up to one large room inside. There still were the two separate entrances and two separate steeples. These two buildings stood like twins, but this arrangement would only be temporary because the plans were to build a larger church which would accommodate all of the members from both churches. The church moving took place in September, just in time for the *Lindeman Sangerforbund* which was held there on October 10, 1902.

O come, let us sing unto the Lord. Let us make a joyful noise to the rock of our salvation.

The reading of this Bible verse from Psalms 95 opened an afternoon of singing as *The Lindeman Sangerforbund* (Choral Union) had its first festival in the twin building which was the United Lutheran Church in Canton.

This festival was named after the Norwegian organist and composer of a vast number of hymns, Ludvig Mathias Lindeman. In his time there was a hymnbook shortage in Norway, referred to as a *Salmebognoden* (hymnbook famine). The Norwegian State Church commissioned a pastor in Telemark, Magnus Landstad, to select hymns for a new hymn book. He had it ready in 1868, and Ludvig Lindeman was given the task of preparing a really professional *koralbook*, or tune book, for Landstad's hymnbook.

It was Ludvig Lindeman, who as organist at *Our Saviour's Church* in Christiania had the role of bringing the singing public to a realization of correct hymn singing. When he took over as organist, the singing in the churches was poor beyond words. His opportunity came when he was commissioned to furnish the *koralbook*, or music, for Landstad's hymnbook. He added a number of his own new melodies, and if sung correctly, they added spirit and interest to the singing. He began by using his new melodies as Preludes and Postludes, playing them in the tempo in which he wished them to be sung, tunes such as *"Built on a Rock the Church Doth Stand"* and *"Praise My Soul, the King of Heaven"*.

Soon Lindeman had his congregation leaving the old tradition of the *dragging* congregational singing, bringing new life and interest into the service.

Lindeman could make his organ laugh for joy, or weep in sorrow, and now he had the whole congregation following him in the spirit of the hymns, and he had composed a vast number of them. His influence spread throughout Norway. Many memorized these hymns, verse after verse. When the pioneers came to America, they brought with them their hymnbook, Luther's Catechism, and the Bible, along with the memorized hymns they had in their hearts; and often they sang as they went about their daily duties.

The hymnbook was one of the pioneer woman's most prized possessions, and each Sunday she carried it with her to church, often wrapped in a clean white handkerchief.

Ludvig M. Lindeman did more to improve congregational singing than anyone else, and he gave to church music a large number of the familiar hymns we sing today.

The *Lindeman Sangerforbund* festival which took place in Canton was a celebration of hymn singing, especially those hymns composed by Ludvig M. Lindeman.

Andrew felt a connection with Lindeman because his organ teacher, Mr. Braein, in Kristiansund, had studied organ under Mr. Lindeman in Christiania.

A splendid audience filled the two Canton churches, now under one roof. It was probably the largest gathering ever in any Canton church. A conservative estimate placed the attendance at six hundred, while a large number were turned away because all the standing room was occupied, and some had to stand outside. The program began at 3 p.m., and lasted nearly two hours. *The Lindeman Choral Union* of 125 voices was composed of various church choirs from Lincoln County, South Dakota, and Lyon County, Iowa. Miss Palma Anderson was the accompanist. The individual choirs rendered selections. These were alternated with numbers by the joint chorus. The Honorable Charles O. Knudson sang a solo. The music was under the direction of A. K. Indseth. There were two choirs from Canton, two from Inwood, Iowa, and choirs from Beaver Creek, Moe, Trinity and Hudson, South Dakota.

For the numbers to be sung by the joint chorus, Andrew chose hymns which Lindeman had composed. All the choirs gathered the week before to practice the numbers. At the practice, when the chorus was singing *Built On A Rock*, Andrew remembered the day his organ teacher, Mr. Braein from Kristiansund, had played this hymn on the organ for him, with all the stops out, and how magnificent it sounded. He asked Miss Anderson to play it on the organ to give the choir members the idea of this. He wanted them to put energy and volume into it, and with 125 voices, it could be accomplished.

> *"Built on a rock the church doth stand,*
> *Even when steeples are falling.*
> *Crumbled have spires in ev'ry land*
> *Bells still are chiming and calling;*
> *Calling the young and old to rest;*
> *But above all the soul distressed,*
> *Longing for rest everlasting."*

Andrew decided to have the hymn, "*Jesus, Priceless Treasure*," sung *a cappella*. "This hymn must be sung devotionally," Andrew reminded them. He worked with each part separately and then he put all the parts together. With that many voices, there was no need for a piano or organ.

> *"Jesus, Priceless Treasure,*
> *Source of purest pleasure,*
> *Truest friend to me."*

Alternating between the individual choir selections, were more of Linde-man's compositions: *For the Beauty of the Earth; How Blessed is the Little Flock*, and *Christ, whose Glory Fills the Skies.*

In closing, the joint choirs would sing *"Care for Me, O God of Grace."*

> *"Care for me, O God of grace, Help me that I never*
> *Anxious, look to future days, But may trust Thee ever.*
> *Care for me and care for mine Every day and hour*
> *Care for ev'ry one of Thine, God of grace and power."*

Rev. P. H. Tetlie made a few final remarks.

After the program, many people came up to Andrew to tell him how much they enjoyed hearing the old familiar songs. One lady told him, "When they sang *Jesus Priceless Treasure* without the piano, it was so beautiful, all of those voices in harmony. I closed my eyes and I imagined that this was what the heavenly chorus would sound like. I had to wipe my eyes, because the tears came, it was so beautiful!"

Her friend said her favorite number was *How Blessed is the Little Flock.* "My mother taught it to me when I was a little girl."

The *Sioux Valley News* reviewed the *Lindeman Sangerforbund* festival, and this is part of what they wrote –

> "The music was all under the direction of A. K. Indseth, who has done more than any other person to raise the standard of church music among the Scandinavians."

The building boom in Canton continued. Men had excavated for five new business places across from the Rudolph Hotel, one building to be for the *Sioux Valley News.* This was called the Syndicate block.

The handsome new Rudolph Hotel was finished in October. It was three stories high and a half block long. It had a dining room, and in the basement was a billiard room. Peter Overseth, the president of the new Farmers State Bank, and several other bachelors made the Rudolph their home.

The *Grieg Sangforening* hadn't met during the summer months, but in the fall they began rehearsing again. They had rented a suite of rooms for their practicing. These were known as the Grieg Hall. Professor Indseth was drilling his twenty singers on some new Skandinavian glees. He was a model conduc-tor, and his Grieg boys appreciated his musical ability and his enthusiasm.

Professor Indseth and his Harrisburg-Dayton Township Band - Circa 1903

Front row - Professor Indseth (4th from right), Berger Indseth (1st on right), Ray Indseth (2nd from right)

Third row - Andrew Indseth Jr. (2nd from left)

Chapter 12

" *I*'m going to spend some time with my music this forenoon, Inger. I'll be in the piano room. There are many melodies dancing around in my head, and I want to get them down on paper. I need to be alone with my piano. Some of these tunes I've had since I lived back in Kristiansund – like the tunes I would hear when I looked at the majestic mountains, or as I watched the strange and mystic midnight sun that didn't set. I want to get this music down on paper and make arrangements so they can be played by an orchestra or a band."

"When you talk about these things, I know what you mean, *Andreas*," Inger said. "There is melody in everything. Some sounds are sad, some exciting, and some only a whisper."

Andrew continued, "You know, when I was young, I remember I would stand by the sea with its crashing waves, and sometimes it sounded like the roll of drums, and sometimes it sounded like the plunks of the bass fiddler as the water splashed on the rocks. When I viewed the mountains, I heard the majestic sounds of trumpets and oboes. Often, when we went mountain climbing, and I looked down upon the world below, I could hear the far-off chorus of clarinets and flutes. I want to put these sounds on paper, and arrange them so others when listening to an orchestra or band that plays them, will know these same feelings, just as if they were there."

"Oh, *Andreas*, you make me homesick for Kristiansund when you talk like that,"

Inger then encouraged him. "You can compose music, *Andreas*, I know you can do it. Just close the door, and the children and I will leave you alone."

Andrew had been doing a lot of music arranging for his bands and orchestras, but he had arranged other people's tunes. Now, he had tunes of his own that he wanted to get on paper. *He wanted to write new music.* Really, it was just like when a person who has some exciting news must share it with someone, so now Andrew had something inside him that he wanted to get out.

* * * * *

In June of 1903, Andrew was out at the Moe community again. For a while he had given up the band there, but now a new band was organized. The interested boys and men bought the creamery building at Moe, which had been for sale. They secured fine nickel-plate instruments, and the creamery would be their band hall. The members now were Hagbart Peterson, Ed Linde, Peter Hegnes, William Odegaard, Anton Bekke, Albert Wilson and Martin Overseth. Andrew was there to help them get going.

Andrew had also been leading a band north of Canton – the Harrisburg-Dayton Township Band. It was one of his best bands. His three sons were members, and the band practiced in the Dayton Township Hall.

For Chautauqua week in July 1903, everyone had been praying for warm weather, and their prayers were answered with summer temperatures. The main attraction that year was Herbert Booth's illustrated lectures on Early Christian Martyrs. The scene of the escape of the mother and baby from Roman soldiers was one of the most beautiful ever presented in moving pictures. The audience gave a responsive "*Thank God*" with the fleeing Christian mother when that brutal Roman soldier fell off the foot bridge, and all hoped he fell to his death.

There was a great crowd at the Chautauqua again that year.

One day in the middle of August, Andrew waited at the Canton depot. His two brothers, John August and Joachim, were to arrive on the train from their homeland of Norway. Andrew had taken the two-seated family carriage so he would have room for them and their baggage.

The Canton depot at this time had much to be desired. There was no waiting room for women and children, nor rest rooms, and often there were large numbers of people standing around waiting for their train connections.

When John August and Joachim stepped off the train, Andrew welcomed them and brought them to his home. Inger and the girls had prepared a delicious hot meal for them – a family favorite from the Indseth brothers' youth – *sildball*. The men had been traveling all day and were hungry. The rest of the family thought it was a treat too to have potato dumplings made with the salted herring.

It wasn't long before the three musical brothers were in the piano room, and they were making music. Andrew had been looking forward to this musical reunion with his brothers.

* * * * *

On Sunday, August 30, 1903, the second *Lindeman Sangerforbund* met at 10:30 a.m. at the Chautauqua grounds. There was a service of singing and preaching. At twelve o'clock, dinner was served on the grounds. At 2:30 p.m., the concert of 100 voices sang selections composed by Ludvig M. Lindeman, and the different choirs from Canton, Inwood, and the Moe and Hudson communities rendered separate numbers. There were over 1000 people present. Pastors Tetlie of Canton, Berge of Inwood and Solberg gave brief addresses.

Andrew was again in charge of the music. This year he chose the following numbers by composer Lindeman. The joint choir opened with "*Praise My Soul, the King of Heaven.*"

Alternating with the various church choirs, were these Lindeman songs, "*Jesus, Jesus, Only Jesus*" and "*Come Ye Faithful, Raise the Strain.*"

A delightful number was "*As the Sunflower Turns in the Morning,*" using Lindeman's *Gift of Grace* melody. It was bright and enjoyable to sing.....

> "*As the sunflower turns in the morning,*
> *To commune with the brightness abroad,*
> *So, my soul, to receive His adorning,*
> *Now, awake, and respond to your God.*"

After the concert and business meeting, the various choirs were given an enjoyable excursion on the Sioux River. Gilbert Dokken, from *Trefoldighed Church* (Trinity), south of Canton, was elected the next president, and he announced that next year's *Lindeman Sangerforbund* would be at his church, the Trinity Church, located east of Moe, which was being rebuilt after the 1902 tornado.

* * * * *

The new Augustana College building was finished in the late summer of 1903. On the second floor was a chapel, which held 350 persons. The inside of the building had been plastered and all the walls painted white. The red granite building was an imposing structure.

At the top of the building was the flagstaff with a beautiful globe. From the top of the square tower, one could look east over into the Lyon County, Iowa, hills, and south way down to Moe.

The United Lutheran Mission Conference met in Canton from October 1 thru 4, of 1903, and at the conclusion, the new Augustana Main building was dedicated. The big tent of Mr. Forrest was secured, and planks were set up to seat 1400. The south wall of the tent was raised where the crowd could stand, and many sat in carriages outside during the exercises.

Andrew again had a part in an important event in Canton. His excellent Harrisburg band opened the meeting, and later the *Grieg Sangforening* sang. To begin, everyone joined in singing *"Vor Gud Han er Saa Fast en Borg"* (A Mighty Fortress is Our God). Rev. Kildahl from St. Olaf College spoke for 45 minutes, and the audience was spellbound. Many old men, young men and women shed tears as the speaker appealed to them from the Word.

The building was dedicated by Rev. H. Dahl, the President of the United Lutheran Church. President Tuve announced the program. There was an offering taken, amounting to $1500. The program closed with *"Gud's Ord det er Vort Arvgegods"* (God's Word is Our Great Heritage). About 3000 people attended.

President Anthony Tuve, and Canton and the surrounding community were rejoicing that their College was going forward. They had emptied their pockets to make this happen.

1903 Lindeman Sangerforbund at Chautauqua auditorium, Canton, SD
Professor Indseth, front row, fourth from right, with the 100 singers from area church choirs.

Inside Chautauqua Auditorium, Canton, South Dakota - 1904

Chapter 13

*J*t was a cold January day outside, but in Inger's kitchen her big black cookstove warmed the room. This morning she had another reason to have a good fire in the stove. She and her daughter Jennie were making *lefse*.

Inger bent over the flour-dusted kitchen table as she rolled one piece of the potato mixture after another into large circles with her special grooved rolling pin. She carefully put each piece onto the *lefse* stick and carried it to Jennie, who stood by the stove and baked the *lefse* on the stove's hot surface. Already they had a stack of finished pieces, which Jennie kept covered with a towel.

Piano sounds came from the music room where Andrew was working. Inger recognized the melody he was playing as the piece he had composed. Now he was making an arrangement for it, so it could be performed by an orchestra.

Andrew's two brothers, who had arrived from Norway last August, were still staying with them. Last fall and during the Christmas season they had jobs clerking in Hanson and Grevlos' General Store downtown, where many Norwegian-Americans shopped. The store had been so busy that at times five extra clerks were needed. Now since the first of the year, business had slowed and they weren't needed, so Joachim and John August had been spending time with Andrew and his musical interests.

Joachim played his violin in the Wendt's Orchestra in Canton, which Andrew directed, and he played his cornet in several of Andrew's bands. John August often attended chorus practices with Andrew and added his fine voice to the choruses, and when they needed another bass fiddle in one of the orchestras, he was there. When Andrew was choosing new pieces for his choruses and bands, the three brothers would often sing through the different parts, or play them with their instruments so Andrew could get an idea of the new piece of music.

Today Joachim and John August were running an errand for Inger. Her coffee supply was very low and she had asked them to go down to the grocery store for her. Last night at Grieg practice, E. C. Hanson had informed Andrew that his store had received a supply of frozen fish, which Inger had been waiting for. In fact, that was the reason Inger and Jennie were making *lefse* today. According to Inger, you couldn't serve fish without *lefse*. The men would pick up the fish for her also.

When Inger had rolled out the last piece, she began the task of cleaning up the kitchen. She cleared off the table and wiped up the flour that had spread around. Picking up the woven rag rug on which she had been standing, she went outside the door to shake the flour from it, only to come in shivering from the low outdoor temperatures.

When daughter Jennie had baked the last piece of *lefse*, she wiped the flour from the surface of the stove, then filled the coffee pot, setting it on the front of the stove to boil.

"Mother, I emptied the coffee can," she informed her mother.

"I know, Jennie. Your Uncles Joachim and John August are getting more at the store."

Inger took off her apron, all covered with flour. When she tried to brush the flour from her sleeve, she noticed that her long dark skirt was dusted with it too.

"Oh, *nei-da*, it is impossible for a person to roll out *lefse* without getting covered with flour. I must change my clothes. You never know when someone might drop in. This afternoon some of your father's students are having lessons."

Before she left the kitchen, she told Jennie, "Butter some pieces of *lefse* for your Uncles to have with their coffee when they get back."

Inger had barely left the room when the door opened, letting in the chilly January air. Joachim and John had returned, and the Indseth's youngest son, Roy, who had been bundled up and was playing outside with the neighbor boys, came in with them.

Young five-year-old Roy flung off his scarves, coat and stocking cap and headed for the stack of *lefse* that Jennie was buttering.

Joachim and John immediately inquired for Andrew, set the groceries down, quickly removed their coats, fur caps, and overshoes and headed for the music room.

Joachim gave a quick knock and entered.

"*Andrew, you've got to hear this! There is sad news from Norway going around downtown today.*"

John August filled in the details - "*The town of Aalesund was practically destroyed by fire a couple of days ago.*"

Andrew was shocked. "What is this you are saying?"

Right away the picture of that seacoast town located south of Kristiansund came into his mind. This was a town so much like Kristiansund. It was also situated on several islands, and its main industry also was *klippfisk.*

"Why, I have been there many times! And I know many people there."

"*Ja,*" Joachim added, "but now there are 10,000 homeless people there... and it's winter!

John August gave more information. "First the church, schoolhouse, shops and three-fourths of the town burned, and then with the brisk wind the latest report said the remaining buildings were on fire, and that the destruction of Aalesund was complete."

Joachim added, "But so far there is no loss of life."

"That's one good thing," Andrew commented.

"Physicians and medical supplies and some tents are being sent from Bergen. Even Germany has loaded up a ship with food, blankets, and all sorts of supplies," Joachim explained. "Downtown they are receiving funds from Cantonites for the fire sufferers in Aalesund. Just today they had collected something like $100, which they were forwarding to the *Skandinavian* in Chicago, who would be sending it on."

Inger had been standing at the door listening to the tragic news from Norway. She kept shaking her head and exclaiming, "*Oh nei-da! Oh nei-da! Oh me, oh my!*"

Andrew shook his head too, and added, "January 23, 1904, was certainly a sad day for Aalesund."

Inger then remembered what she had come for, "I want to tell you that Jenny has the coffee ready, and you boys better come and sample the *lefse.*"

Andrew left the piano bench and headed for the door, "*Ja, jeg har kaffetørst* (I am thirsty for coffee). What about you, Joachim and John?"

As they walked along to the kitchen, Andrew expressed the feelings of all of them as he said, "When I think of the poor people in Aalesund, it makes me very thankful that we have a warm house...and food."

His footsteps quickened as he added, "*Why, we even have lefse!*"

*   *   *   *   *

In February of 1904, Andrew and Inger and their family moved to a farm east of Canton. The owner of the farm, Halvor Martin, had moved into Canton, and Andrew's two oldest sons, Ray and Andrew, Jr., were going to farm it, with the help of their younger brother, Berger, and advice from Mr. Martin.

Halvor had sold his team of workhorses to them and was letting them use his old machinery so they could get started farming. The boys weren't new to farming because for many summers they had worked on farms, and Ray had worked for Halvor Martin this past year.

"It's a nice big house, Mother," the boys had told her, "with plenty of bedrooms for our family. And a big dining room. It's only a mile and a half from town. A person could easily walk to town if he had to. Our younger sisters can attend a country school close by."

Purchasing some pigs and a couple of milk cows made the boys bona fide farmers.

"This should work out well, "Andrew thought to himself. "This will keep the family together, instead of having each one moving away to different jobs."

That way Andrew could keep his family band intact. The boys were getting to be excellent musicians. He was proud of them, and he relied on them to be part of his bands and the Wendt orchestra.

"But you boys remember that I am not a farmer! I have enough to do with my music," he told them.

Now they were all settled in the peace and quiet of country life. The boys were excited about their new enterprise, and they weren't afraid of hard work. Besides their farm work, they spent a lot of time with their music. Joachim and John August had moved out to the farm with them.

It was time for the annual concert of the *Grieg Sangforening*, the eleventh one. It was held in the Canton Armory Hall on March 2, 1904. The sudden change in the weather kept a number of people from attending, but in spite of the cold wind, a good audience was present.

The Grieg men were smartly dressed in dark trousers, white shirts, ties and navy jackets and they all wore jaunty sea captain caps. The program opened with a rendition of "*Norge Norge*", accompanied by the Wendt Orchestra.

Four ladies joined four of the men to make a mixed octet that sang "*The Sea, Wondrous Sea*".

"*Naar Fjordene Blaaner*" by the entire chorus was well received and they responded with an encore.

A ladies' octet sang "*The Blue Bells of Scotland*", after which the Grieg men presented "Feltvagten" as the closing number of Part I.

Part II opened with a selection, "*Artist's Dream*", by the Wendt Orchestra, and the orchestra graciously responded to an encore.

"*Sjømann*" (*The Sailor*) by the Grieg Chorus was the second number.

For variety from all the vocal numbers, Professor Olaf Fossen presented a piano solo - Edvard Grieg's *"Wedding Day"*. It was charmingly performed, and he was compelled to respond with an encore.

"Robin Adair" by a gentlemen octet was a very pleasing number, which was also encored. The Grieg men sang *"Kari aa Mari"*, and then they joined with the orchestra to conclude the evening's entertainment with the national hymn *"America"*.

Andrew as leader of both the *Grieg Sangforening* and the Wendt Orchestra was pleased with the evening performance. He was now beginning his twelfth year as the leader and instructor of the *Grieg Sangforening*.

$$* \quad * \quad * \quad * \quad * \quad *$$

Inger was standing by the kitchen window when she noticed a lone robin hopping about in the yard. It was only March nineteenth, and rather cold weather for birds, but she thought it must mean that Spring was on its way. She was enjoying farm life. When she looked to the east and south, she could see the steep hills along the Sioux River. One hill stood high enough to be made into a ski jump. Everywhere she had lived previously in South Dakota, the land had been so flat. She had missed the mountains of Norway.

Inger became very excited one day when she caught sight of seagulls following the plow as the boys did their spring work, turning up the fresh soil. The familiar birds brought back memories of the flocks of seagulls around Kristiansund.

In spring the little wild plum trees growing along the fence lines burst into bloom, and in May, the big apple tree by the house was covered with dainty scented blossoms. Now Inger spent some time outside each day taking care of the hens. It was so nice to have fresh eggs every day. The girls helped with the chicken chores, and Inger enjoyed watching the hens that had little chicks trailing behind them as they moved about the yard.

The morning of July 4, 1904, the boys finished the chores early and Inger and Andrew's family were all getting ready to celebrate the holiday.

The boys - Ray, Andy, Jr., Berger and Uncle Joachim came into the kitchen dressed in their new white band uniforms with the gold braid and gold buttons. Today the Canton Band was going to play for the patriotic program at the Chautauqua. Andrew soon appeared in his white uniform too.

"You fellows must be careful that you don't rub against the buggy and get your new uniforms soiled," Inger cautioned. "Remember that white shows everything."

Inger gave a quick glance at each of them and pronounced, "You all look great."

The band members had to leave early so they would have time to tune up before the forenoon session of the Chautauqua opened.

Daughter Inez's friend, Bert Gallahan, was coming to pick her up, and Jennie was joining some of her classmates.

Brother John August, Inger and the rest of the family were going to attend this patriotic event at the Chautauqua also. John August would drive the surrey and transport them to the Chautauqua grounds along the beautiful Sioux River in lower Canton. The children had their swimming suits along. They planned to swim in the afternoon.

Inger, Malinda, Florence, Josephine and Roy found seats in the big Chautauqua building. They were going to take in the forenoon program. John August sat with some of his men friends.

This Chautauqua building was many-sided, and almost round. The stage was on the west side, and there were screened openings all the way around to let in the summer breezes, with canvas awnings that could be lowered when it rained. Posts were situated here and there to support the structure. A center section of the roof, or dome, was raised to a higher level with little windows all around, letting in additional light. On the main floor, there was tiered seating for 3000 people or more.

Inger looked around as the people were assembling. Many were finely dressed - the men in their suits, white shirts, carrying their sporty straw hats, and the women in fashionable white linen suits with ankle-length skirts, dainty white blouses with tucks and lace, long dark skirts, and fancy hats. For Canton society, the days of Chautauqua were some of the main social events of the year.

Andrew's Canton Band opened the Independence Day event with patriotic numbers and marches. The band looked so fine in their new white uniforms with the gold braid and made a very good impression.

Following the music, the first person on the forenoon program was a gentleman who recited the *Declaration of Independence*.

Then onto the stage came a young woman, dressed in plain homespun clothes, her bonnet hanging down her back. She was portraying the daughter of a Revolutionary War soldier. Acting her part, she read a letter from her purported soldier father that told about the Army's problems. He had been fighting in the Connecticut Infantry Company under George Washington.

When she went into detail about the difficult life of the women who were left to do the farming and care for the livestock while the men went off to war, she got the audience's sympathy as she told how frightened the families sometimes were when one of the battles being fought came close to their farm, or when sickness came to their families. The audience seemed moved as she told about the Revolutionary War life. Her portrayal was very enlightening for Inger, who was learning of the early history of the United States.

To conclude the forenoon program, Katharine Gemmill sang a solo and Andrew's band played several more marches. Then it was time for the meeting to break for the noon meal.

Inger and the children didn't attend the afternoon session. After they had eaten the picnic lunch she had brought along, the children took their swimming suits and went to change in the bath houses. Inger kept their clothes while they swam and played on the Sioux River beach. She found a nice shady spot under the trees where she sat and visited with some other mothers.

Professor Indseth and his handsome white-uniformed Canton Band opened the afternoon program. This was followed by an oration.

There was a big crowd this fourth day of the 1904 Chautauqua. Nearly 3,000 people attended and enjoyed the magnificent patriotic program. All afternoon the sound of firecrackers being discharged could be heard around town. Both young and old celebrated the Fourth of July in those days.

Day five of the Chautauqua was slated for a big debate. The topic was... *Should the location of the South Dakota capitol be changed*? During its winter session the State Legislature had brought up the subject of changing the state capitol from Pierre to Mitchell, and the people were going to vote on it in the fall.

In the debate Pierre flunked out and only sent a delegation of forty people to the Chautauqua event, while Mitchell came rolling into Canton with eight train coaches loaded to the steps. The Pierre delegation said the capitol should remain at Pierre, and they hoped now to round up voters again. But the Mitchell delegation presented a good argument for their city. One of their reasons was that Pierre was not as accessible as Mitchell, with Mitchell's good train service and good highway. It was even questioned how Pierre got the capitol fourteen years ago in the campaign of 1890. There were hints of fraud and bribery.

Heated discussions continued even after the Chautauqua and throughout the summer and fall. Many of the people in southeastern South Dakota were for Mitchell. The editor of the newspaper wrote....

> "Mitchell, Mitchell, God bless you! It's the only place that meets
> the requirements of all the people. It's central."

Later in the fall, when all the ballots were counted, Pierre kept their capitol!

*   *   *   *   *

The *Grieg Sangforening* was like one big family and they were concerned for one another, celebrating together at joyous times in their members' lives.

On July 23,1904, the Grieg Chorus held a reception to honor A. N. Bragstad, one of their members, and his new bride. Everyone enjoyed the happy event, which included toasts, speeches, food and singing. An announcement was made that now the organization had only one lone bachelor – G. G. Satrum.

Chapter 14

*A*t the beginning of the summer of 1904, Andrew had reminded himself that it was time to line up the music for the annual *Lindeman Sangerforbund*. This year it was to be held ten and a half miles south of Canton, (two miles east of Moe), at the Trinity church, on July twenty-third. Andrew again studied Lindeman's compositions, and found some that the *Sangerforbund* hadn't previously performed.

When Andrew thought of the hymn composer, Ludvig Mathias Lindeman, Andrew always remembered his organ teacher, Christian Braein, playing the powerful music of Lindeman's *"Built on a Rock"* in the Kristiansund Kirke (church). Andrew felt a special connection with this composer because this famous man had been Mr. Braein's organ teacher. This year Andrew decided that the chorus of one hundred singers would join in the singing of

> *My Soul, Now Bless Thy Maker*
> *Come to Calvary's Holy Mountain*
> *Savior, Like a Shepherd Lead Us*
> *Abide Among Us, We Implore Thee*

Gilbert Dokken, the 1904 president of the *Lindeman Sangerforbund*, had been a busy man as he made the physical arrangements for the organization's annual concert at the Trinity Church, where he was a member.

The Trinity Church had just been rebuilt after being destroyed in the 1902 tornado, and it still wasn't completely finished. Already it was a beautiful church, but it just didn't have room for the one to two thousand people who would gather for the Lindeman concert, so Dokken rented Mr. Forrest's large tent. He had a platform built for the piano and singers.

The one hundred singers were coming from two Canton church choirs, two Inwood church choirs, and choirs from Moe, Trinity and Hudson churches. Many singers had a long way to travel by horse and buggy so Dokken made plans for a grand picnic at noon in the Paul Thompson Gubrud grove, one-half mile north of the church. A stand was set up, serving pop and lemonade, and Pastor Nummedal, the pastor for Moe and Trinity, gave a short sermon for those who couldn't attend their own church that Sunday.

In his simple heart-searching way, Pastor Nummedal addressed the audience, "*Kjaere dere*" (My dear ones). This was the way he always spoke to his congregations.

> "My heart is steadfast, O God,
> I will sing and make music with all my soul. Ps. 108:1"

He continued.... "There is some music that can be sung here on earth, which according to the Bible will someday be sung in heaven. It is known as the NEW SONG".

Pastor Nummedal then opened his Bible and read Psalms 40:2, 3:

> "He lifted me out of the slimy pit, out of the mud and mire; he set
> my feet on a rock and gave me a firm place to stand. He put a NEW
> SONG in my mouth, a hymn of praise to our God."

"*Kjaere dere*, my singers: This new song is a beautiful song we can sing when we have the *joy of our salvation*. Praise God for what He has done for us!"

After the picnic, two photographers lined up the big crowd at the edge of the grove and took a picture of them. This would be made into scrolls, or rolled-up photographs.

The Sunday appointed for the annual singing festival turned out to be an ideal July day, and something like 2000 people were present to enjoy the song festival. Mr. Dokken received many compliments for his successful efforts for the festival.

The music was again under the direction of Professor Indseth. The numbers of Ludvig M. Lindeman music that he chose to have sung were performed by the one hundred voices, and the various choirs presented individual numbers besides.

The singing was superb because the choirs entered into the spirit of the occasion with all the fervor of musical enthusiasts. It was a beautiful manifestation of the power of music.

The new officers of the Lindeman Sangerforbund for the coming year were.... President Henry Moen, Inwood, Iowa; Vice President G. G. Dokken, Hudson, SD; Secretary, Ida Scheie, Inwood, Iowa; Treasurer, Rosen Ingebretson, Fairview, SD. Next year's session was tentatively planned to be held in Canton.

*   *   *   *   *

During the summer Andrew had provided the same band music to both his Canton Band and the Inwood Band. The members of both bands had been working on the same pieces, and now arrangements had been made to have joint concerts. The first one was to be held in Inwood.

The last of August, the Canton boys joined the Inwood band in Inwood. The united group numbered thirty-two musicians, and they gave the Lyon County, Iowa, friends a grand musical concert. A similar concert was planned for Wednesday evening, September 2, when the Inwood band would join the Canton band for a concert in Canton.

"I have a busy day today," Andrew announced to Inger, as he filled her in. "I need to make a trip into town to the newspaper office to get the upcoming Canton-Inwood joint band concert advertised, and then I have violin lessons in Beloit." He grabbed his hat and told her, "It is such a nice day, I think I'll go on foot. I need some exercise."

When Andrew got to the newspaper office, located across from the Rudolph hotel, there was a flock of people standing out in the street. As he got closer, he saw what the attraction was – *a new automobile.* A man informed him that it belonged to a Dr. Opland from Beresford. The Doctor had just made the thirty mile run from Beresford in sixty minutes.

Andrew went into the editor's office to give him the upcoming band concert information, and while he was there a Mr. A. B. Andrews came in. *This man was so excited.* He had just been on a mile-a-minute ride with Dr. Opland out in the country and he wanted to tell the editor about it. Andrew listened to his account.

Mr. A. B. Andrews patted down his straggly hairs, and explained, "One thing, my hair wasn't where it ought to be when I got back from the spin." He then went on to describe his ride....

> "The section lines looked like street corners; trees and fence posts made a blur against the beautiful background of green, which afterwards I found out to be cornfields.
>
> "Riding out in the country can be a beautiful picture," said Mr. Andrews, "but a mile-a-minute gives one a poor chance to admire the beauty of nature....or shoot a festive prairie chicken which we passed in its mad flight to escape.
>
> "A jack rabbit turned into the road. It was so scared when it heard the auto horn, it just laid his long ears back, and how he did

bound along! A ways down the road here lay the rabbit, dead of a heart attack.

"A man who has not gone through the country atmosphere at the rate of a mile a minute has no idea what it means. You just sit and brace yourself and feel that you may be in heaven before you know it."

The editor asked him if he would go again, and he exclaimed, "No, thank you!" He then added, "I may one day get myself an automobile...but you won't find me driving over thirty miles an hour."

When Andrew Indseth walked out of the news office, he stopped to look over this machine. He would have to tell his brothers and his boys about this *automobile* and this man's ride...*but it probably would be in next week's newspaper.*

Next, Andrew headed for Beloit. After the violin session, he decided that he'd take the short-cut home, following the railroad tracks and crossing over the railroad bridge. As he walked along, he was reviewing all the upcoming activities on his calendar. On the first of August, a group of twenty young ladies in the Canton area had organized a band, and had asked him to be their instructor and leader. He would have to order some music for them. They would be an attraction, but it would take some time to get them ready for a public performance. And he was working with the Moe Band again and there were plans to go with them to Hudson Saturday night and entertain the people on the streets down there.

The news was out that the famous band conductor and composer, John Phillip Sousa, was scheduled to be in Mitchell, South Dakota, at the Corn Palace Exposition with his sixty piece band the week of September 26, 1904. Tuesday, September 27, had been set as Sioux Falls and Canton Days. The invitation was sent out for several musical organizations from Lincoln and Minnehaha Counties to participate that day. Special trains would be running all week. Andrew felt that the Wendt Orchestra would be able to prepare some numbers for this. He would have to bring it up to them and see if they wanted to perform.

Andrew had been so deep in thought that he hadn't noticed that a train was coming until he heard its whistle. He looked back. It wasn't too far away, and he was only half way across the railroad bridge. He realized that he wouldn't have time to get across, so he knew he had only one choice....he would have to jump! And jump he did! There wasn't much water beneath, but he landed safely and his rapidly beating heart finally slowed down. He pulled himself up on the bank, all wet and muddy, and headed for home.

When Inger saw him, she put her hands on her hips and shook her head.

"*Nei, Andreas*, what happened to you?" But when she heard of his close brush with death, she was very thankful he had escaped the train and she got clean clothes for him. This was the second time Andrew had come home after being soaked in the Sioux River.

*   *   *   *   *

Early Tuesday morning, September 27, 1904, the members of the Wendt Orchestra gathered at the Canton depot with their instruments to board the train for Mitchell. The violins, cornets, trombones, clarinets, flutes, bass fiddle and drum all were loaded on the train. Six members of the Indseth family were part of the orchestra – sons Ray and Berger with their clarinets, son Andy, Jr. with his trombone, Professor Indseth with his baton, and Andrew's brothers, Joachim with his violin and John August with the bass fiddle. They were going to play at the Mitchell Corn Palace. The orchestra had had many practices to prepare for this important performance. They were aware that the famous John Phillip Sousa would most likely hear them.

Andrew decided that the number they had performed at the Grieg Chorus winter concert, entitled "*The Artist's Dream*" could be used, and they worked on that and one other number, but Andrew wondered what they should use for their third number. One day Andrew had been listening as his son, Andy, Jr., practiced the classical piece, "*The Holy City*", on his trombone. Andrew decided this would be a good selection for their third number.

The Wendt Orchestra was slated to play right after Sousa's afternoon band concert. The Canton musicians took their places and the group performed very well. Then it was time for Andrew, Jr.'s solo. His father went to the piano to accompany him. The tones of the trombone came out rich, mellow and clean. Andrew, Jr. continued throughout the long piece, not getting winded, and playing with feeling. He performed "*The Holy City*" the best he had ever played it.

After Andy finished, the orchestra members began to gather up their music and instruments when the famous composer and band leader, John Philip Sousa, walked over to them.

"Your concert was very nice," he said.

Then he headed for Andrew, Jr., "Your trombone solo was excellent, young man. I would like to use you in my band."

Andrew, Jr. didn't know what to say....only, "Thank you, sir."

Then Sousa added, "I know you can't make such a big decision at such short notice, so you go home and think about it. I'll get in touch with you in a few weeks and you can let me know what you decide."

Andrew was very proud of his son. To be approached by Sousa to be a member of his famous band was an honor. The Professor felt it was an honor for himself also because he had trained and taught his son so well. He had always known that Andy had special musical talent.

The Canton group stayed to listen to the evening concert of Sousa's band and then returned on the special evening train to Canton. It was an unforgettable experience to have played for the famous Sousa.

The next few weeks the decision to be made by Andrew, Jr. was discussed over and over.

"I feel that Andy isn't old enough to go out into the world, traveling day after day, week after week, month after month," his mother Inger said. Then she added, "Not only here in America, but into Europe, and other parts of the world. He is just eighteen. I think a person should be twenty-one before taking on a job like that."

His brother Ray spoke up, "If Andy goes, we'll have to give up the farm. I can't farm all by myself. And then we'll have to move back into town."

His father didn't like to tell his son he couldn't join John Phillip Sousa's band. After all, this was an opportunity of a lifetime.... but what would happen to his own Indseth family band? His son was needed in the bands he directed, and in the Wendt Orchestra. When it came right down to it, Andrew was hoping that his son would say *"No"* to Sousa. Perhaps when he was older, he would get the opportunity again.

How did Andrew, Jr. himself feel? He knew that this would be an adventure, but it would be a strange life, with all the traveling and performing several times a day. Perhaps he hadn't been trained as well as many of the other musicians, and he would have trouble keeping up. And he didn't know any of these other band members. He had to admit that he was comfortable with the life he had in Canton and the music opportunities he had here. Besides that, he knew that his father depended on him.

When the letter addressed to *Mr. Andrew Indseth, Jr., Canton, South Dakota* arrived in the mail, with the invitation again from John Phillip Sousa to join his organization, Andrew Jr. had made up his mind. His answer was.........

Dear Mr. Sousa,

Thank you for your invitation to join your organization. I feel it has been an honor to have been asked. Both I and my family have spent much time weighing this decision, and I am afraid I have to say "NO" because I feel I am needed here at this time.

Again, thank you for honoring me with your invitation.

Sincerely yours,

Andrew Indseth, Jr.

* * * * * *

In the fall of 1904, G. G. Satrum, the bachelor, was elected president of the Grieg Sangforening for the coming year. On December 2, the Chorus had a banquet to honor their new president. The wives were invited, too, and this was their Christmas party. A Christmas tree had been set up in the Grieg Hall and the room had been decorated with Christmas decorations.

After the meal, the Grieg Chorus members and their wives enjoyed the old Norwegian custom of walking around the Christmas tree and singing songs. They sang "*Jeg er Saa Glad Hver Julekveld*" (I Am So Glad Each Christmas Eve); " *Du Grønne Glitrende Tre*" (You Green, Glittering Tree); "*Glade Jul*" (Silent Night), and other Christmas songs. All the men and women knew the verses of these songs by heart – *in the Norwegian language*.

There was always good conversation when the group got together. Several of the members of the Chorus had been to the carpentry shop which Mr. Satrum and his brother ran, and they had seen the Satrum Brothers' latest artistic projects – the beautiful pulpit, and altar for the new Trinity Church, with the intricate carving and style. The Satrum brothers received much praise for their work. These pieces were almost ready to be installed in their new church home.

While on the subject of artistic projects, one of the men mentioned, "You must go around and see the beautiful store windows in town this Christmas. Our friend, Adolph Bragstad here, has his shoe store window beautifully decorated like a Cinderella fairyland, with palaces fit for a fairy and all her beautiful slippers. You all must stop and see it. This year the storekeepers have really outdone themselves."

Dr. Wendt Orchestra - 1904

Back row - Professor Indseth with baton (1st on left), Berger Indseth (2nd from left),
Andrew Indseth Jr (4th from left), Ray Indseth (5th from left), brother Joachim Indseth (5th from left)

Chapter 15

O ut they go! Out they go! To North Dakota! In 1905, the front pages of the newspapers were full of advertisements of cheap land in North Dakota. Many people were traveling north to investigate. Some were buying farms for their sons. Many new towns were being established, and now there were many business opportunities in North Dakota. About this time Andrew's brother, John August Indseth, decided to move on. He married a girl named Emma and they moved north. They made their home on a farm near Robinson, North Dakota.

The year of 1905 was a great year for Professor Andrew Indseth. From January through December, he was able to showcase the organizations he was leading.

It began on January 20 with Canton's Annual Music Festival, which was held at the Opera House. That night the building was packed, with fifty to seventy-five persons standing, and that night the Wendt Orchestra, led by Professor Indseth, gave ample proof that the orchestra had made splendid progress. They opened the program with the numbers they had performed in Mitchell the previous September, and for an encore they brought one of Sousa's beautiful compositions, which had been so much admired when the March King played it at the Corn Palace in September.

The Grieg Chorus was superb as usual. Among the songs they sang were "*Brude Ferden*" and "*Jeg Vil Verge Mitt Land*". Andrew Indseth, Jr. presented the trombone solo, "*The Holy City*", which he had played in Mitchell.

Dr. Wendt announced the final overture, which was performed by the orchestra. It was entitled "*The Midnight Sun*", and it was the number composed by their leader, Professor Indseth. This was the music that Andrew had been working on. Wendt explained that it was away up on a mountain crag where one could see this glorious sun circle that the composer had felt the glory of the scene – a world's end, as it were - and there in his heart the music of the midnight sun burst forth in glorious unison with God's glorious painting for the human eyes.

The audience was swept along with the music as they too sensed the glory of the midnight sun as the violins, cellos, flutes, clarinets, trumpets, trombones, and bass fiddle played the exciting melody. Indseth's composition drew forth acclaim and the Wendt Orchestra was awarded high praise. It was a GREAT concert.

In January and February of 1905, the weather was very cold and there was much snow. On February 1, it was 42 degrees below zero. The bitter cold reached from Canada to the Gulf. Coal dealers couldn't keep a supply of coal on hand, and they were always awaiting their next shipment. But Spring came early in 1905. In March the snow began to melt, and soon the frozen ground was thawing. This made the dirt roads a fright, with mud holes and deep ruts, and even buggies became stuck in the mud.

March 10 was the date for the Moe Band concert at the Iverson Opera House in Hudson, South Dakota. Andrew, Joachim, Ray, Andrew, Jr., and Berger boarded the train in Canton for the trip to Hudson. The rest of the band members, living in the Moe area, had to plow through the mud with their horses and buggies to get to Hudson.

The band played marches and overtures, and the program included duets and solos. The Hudson newspaper editor wrote that the Moe Band had greatly improved and both Norway Township and Professor Indseth could be proud of it.

Brother Joachim played a violin solo, which was encored *twice*. The splendid tenor voice of Gilbert Dokken charmed all the hearers with his solo, and then he was joined with Martin Mortenson for a duet. Joachim, with his sporty mustache, was a comical gent. He brought down the house with a spe-cialty song about taking care of the baby while Mama had gone to the Physical Culture Class. The words weren't always understood, but the actions plainly showed what he was singing about.

Because the roads were so bad, the concert was not well attended, but those who came were treated to an evening of special entertainment.

Telephone lines had been set up in the rural areas surrounding Canton and most farms were getting hooked into it. Now it was so convenient for those having telephones to ring the telephone operator and have her contact the person to whom they wished to speak, instead of harnessing up the horses and driving to their house. This operator was supposed to have the answers for everything – the time of all the trains, and if a train was late, and how many minutes behind. Often she was asked the time of day, and was supposed to know where the fire was. The entertainment of many farm families that cold snowy winter, was to rubber, or listen in, on their neighbor's phone calls. But when spring came, one farm woman sadly stated, *"Now we are so busy with the spring work, we don't have time to listen."*

Easter was right around the corner, and the Canton newspapers were full of advertising of apparel for both men and women. Tom Sexe advertised custom-made men's suits for fifteen dollars, Puckett-Pidcoe Company showed stylish women's suits and fancy blouses in whole page advertisements, and the millinery shops in town advertised spring grand openings.

"Mother, have you seen the advertisements for the spring millinery openings in town?" Inez asked her mother. "I think you and I and Jenny should go into Canton and take in one of them. They all sound special. Jenny and I want to help you find a new hat."

During the month of April, the three millinery shops in Canton held Spring Openings. Mrs. Milliman had already held hers. Her shop had been beautifully decorated with fresh flowers. English violets from the southland were the decoration for one window, and the other window held carnations in all their varied shades. The sweet breath of spring prevailed the atmosphere there.

The Indseth ladies decided to attend Helga Hage's opening, which was the second week of the month. The boys harnessed up the horse for them, hitched it to the buggy, and the ladies were on their way. When they entered Helga Hage's store, they imagined they were in Japan. There were Japanese lanterns, umbrellas, and huge Japanese vases filled with palms and flowers, and the ladies walked on Japanese matting. A Japanese screen confronted them behind which a sweet voice induced them to peek and they discovered a dainty young lady, who smilingly offered them a fragrant cup – not of tea, but of coffee – for in Canton everybody drank coffee. As the ladies sipped and smiled and chatted, they felt Miss Hage's millinery openings were one thing they would never want to miss. Helga and her assistant, Gennivieve Buckin, had been to Minneapolis on a purchasing trip. Gennivieve would trim and adorn the beautiful creations for the customers.

Inger chose a black finely woven straw, and the girls had Gennivieve add a gorgeous silk flower and some draping. "Oh, Mother, it looks so nice!" Her daughters were pleased with it.

A third millinery shop was owned by a Mrs. Riggins. In the newspaper she was quoted as assuring the public that her opening would surpass the two preceding ones.

When the three Indseth ladies were in town, they also looked at dresses at the Puckett-Pidcoe store. Inez had just informed her parents that she and Bert were planning to be married in the summer. "I want to have the wedding at home, out on the farm," she said. "We don't have any relatives around here to invite, so it will be a small gathering. Just a few friends, and Bert's immediate family." The wedding was tentatively being planned for June. Inez would need a special dress for that special occasion, and she wanted to check out the dresses at Pucketts.

After they returned home, they showed their father what they had purchased, and had their mother model her new hat. "But," Inez remarked, "the sidewalks were awful today! Those tobacco-chewers spit on the sidewalks, and a lady has to watch where she steps. If she doesn't lift her long skirt, it will be dragged through that unsanitary stuff. Someone should do something about that!"

At their annual Grieg business meeting in February, someone suggested that the *Grieg Sangforening* should sponsor a *Syttende Mai* (May 17) celebration. The men became very excited about the idea. Another member suggested that they have it at the large auditorium at the Chautauqua grounds. "It can be a big picnic, with food, and speeches and music."

The Grieg members went ahead with the arrangements and plans, and on May 17, people began to gather at the Chautauqua grounds. The attendees could have a picnic dinner in the park with refreshment booths set up with cold drinks, sandwiches, and various other foods. The charge for the program was fifteen cents for adults, and the children could enter free.

The speakers were Reverend S. J. Nummedal, pastor at the Moe Church, and three lawyers and judges from Canton – the Honorable Charles O. Knudson, who was a Grieg member, the Honorable C. B. Kennedy, and the Honorable A. R. Brown.

Knudson reminded the audience of the reason for the celebration. On May 17, 1814, Norway wanted to be independent after being under Denmark's rule for 400 years, so some of their leaders got together and wrote a Constitution. They loosely followed the United States Constitution. *But the Swedish army appeared*! (Denmark had traded Norway to Sweden.) Finally Sweden agreed that Norway would be allowed to retain this new Constitution on the condition that the Swedish King would remain the King of Norway also. A limited monarchy was introduced. The Parliament (*Storting*) would allocate monies and make laws, and the King would exercise his authority through a government. The Norwegians were happy to have their own Constitution, but underneath there still was the desire to be independent.

President Tuve of the Augustana College, gave a dialect address in *Valdresmal*, and Mrs. Adolph Bragstad gave a reading. Interspersed between the speeches and addresses was music by the *Grieg Sangforening* and the Wendt Orchestra. There was a large crowd, and the flag of Norway, with its red, white and blue, waved beside America's red, white and blue, and the many people there celebrated their roots and the Norwegian blood that flowed in their veins. It was Norway's Constitution Day.

Meanwhile, in the country of Norway, important conferences were going on.

Now Norway was standing up for its rights. It had asked Sweden to let it become an independent country. Finally the terms of separation were accepted and the Karlstad Agreement for dissolution of the old union was to be voted on.

When Norwegians living in America heard about this development, they felt their native land, when it became independent, should become a republic instead of a monarchy. Many wrote to their relatives in Norway to encourage this. Other countries were interested also. It was rumored that Emperor William of Germany would like to get a German on the throne of Norway, but Norwegian-Americans thought Norway would look better with a Norwegian President than a German King.

On August 13, 1905, the question of separation from Sweden was voted on in Norway, and the result was 368,000 votes in favor of dissolution of the Norway-Swedish union, while only 184 voted in favor of continuing the union. Norway and Sweden parted in peace, agreed on the terms of separation, and the danger of war was passed.... *but would Norway become a republic or have a king*? That's what Andrew and other Norwegian-Americans asked each other.

In October, the Norwegian Storting by a vote of 101 to 16 accepted the Karlstad Agreement for dissolution of the old union, and gave Premier Mickelsen authority to negotiate with Prince Karl of Denmark for the throne. *None but a Scandinavian prince could be accepted for kingship.* Everyone was agreed on that.

Music Jubilee Bands - 1905

First row - Berger Indseth with drum (5th from left) Second row - Professor Indseth (4th from right),
Ray Indseth (7th from right) Fourth row - brother Joachim with mustache (3rd from right), Charley Eckley (9th from right)
Fifth row - Martin Overseth (2nd from right), Anton Bekke (3rd from right), Herman Johnson (7th from right)
Back row - Andrew Indseth Jr. (1st on left), Tony Overseth (2nd from left)

Chapter 16

I t was a busy June morning for Inger. Today was daughter Inez's wedding day.

"Ray and Andy, you boys take the wagon and go down to Monson's berry farm south of Canton and pick up the strawberries I ordered. On the way back you'll have to stop in Canton at Skartvedt's ice house and get some chunks of ice. I will get the ice cream mixture ready so when you get back you boys can freeze the ice cream."

Inger had baked two cakes, which she was going to decorate with whipped cream and strawberries. Yesterday she and Jennie had made *lefse*, and Inger had baked some of her special graham bread.

Florence and Josephine were picking bouquets of lilacs to set around the house. These would give a sweet fragrance to the rooms. Inger went outside and chose some peonies for an arrangement for the festive table she was setting.

Last night Inger and Andrew had shared their feelings about their oldest child leaving home.

"I am happy for Inez," Inger said, "but I am sad that she will be moving so far away. We won't see her very often."

"The train goes to North Dakota every day," Andrew reminded her. "Remember we were even younger when we left our home town for far away Christiania.

Then Andrew added, "Bert is a good man and the business he is going into at Washburn sounds like a good opportunity for him."

"I do hope it will be nice weather tomorrow," Inger said.

The afternoon of the wedding day the wedding couple's young friends, and Bert's family arrived, along with Carl and Ragna Christiansen, Andrew and Inger's friends from Sioux Falls. Rev. Tetlie, the pastor from Canton, came out and performed the wedding ceremony.

During the meal after the ceremony Joachim played soft violin music while the people ate. It was a happy gathering. Andrew and Inger now had a son-in-law, and their daughter had changed her name to Mrs. Filbert Andrew Gallahan.

Several days later Andrew and Inger went along to the depot to see Inez and Bert off to their new home in Washburn, North Dakota.

A week later, the Canton Band boys, under the direction of Andrew, gave their June 1905 summer concert. It had been very successful, and many compliments had been paid them.

Afterwards the Canton Band boys, still in their attractive white uniforms, gathered at the Grevlos and Son store. As a reward for Gus Fowles and Ole Hokenstad's fine duet, which had been such a hit at the concert, and been encored, Mathias Grevlos promised to set up cigars for all the band, and that was what he did. The band boys enjoyed themselves, and Professor Indseth was happy.

On Labor Day, 1905, a wonderful thing was happening. A new bridge had been built over the Sioux River, connecting the road between Canton and Inwood, and on Labor Day it was to be dedicated. This bridge had been needed for some time because the river ford at the bridge site was dangerous and sometimes too deep for passage. Andrew certainly was aware of this because he had had a bad experience with it.

Many came out for the Canton-Inwood bridge dedication. By 3 p.m. there were 1000 people present. Andrew would be one person who would greatly appreciate this new bridge because he would be traveling over it every week as he attended the Inwood Band and Orchestra practices.

Andrew was very busy preparing for a special event now. He and members of his bands and chorus were making plans for a Grand Concert for the Fall, with all the musical organizations he was instructing taking part.

He began practicing with the four bands – Harrisburg-Dayton Township, Inwood, Iowa, Canton and Moe, and had them all working on the same scores. The plans called for a parade in the afternoon before the joint band concert, and in the evening the singing groups and orchestra would perform. This was a big undertaking and Andrew wanted it to be a success.

Every week Andrew went out to Moe to practice with the band boys there. Martin and Anton Overseth usually accompanied him. Anton was clerking in the Lybarger Store in Canton now, and Martin was making arrangements for a new business venture in Canton. The rest of the Moe Band members were Carl and Hagbart Peterson, Albert Wilson, Albert Grane, Gust and Louie Dokken, Anton Bekke, Ben Skorheim, Charlie Eckley, Herman Johnson and Magnus Fylling. These practices were a time of getting together with old friends and enjoying a social good time. But Andrew made the boys work too.

"We must practice marching," Andrew told them. "Think of what a bad impression we will make if we just straggle along, so we should start practicing marching tonight. You boys need to know several marching pieces by heart because you'll have to play without sheet music when you are marching."

When Wednesday, November 5, 1905, arrived, all the members of Professor Indseth's bands gathered in Canton for the memorable Indseth Musical Jubilee. They came from Inwood, Harrisburg, Moe and Canton. Ray, Andy, Berger and Joachim were there, as they played with several of these bands. Shortly after noon the musical day began with a parade. It was headed by a platoon of guardsmen as escorts for the four bands, led by Lieutenant Way and Lieutenant Eneboe, and under the proud leadership of Professor Indseth. The men marched up Main Street and wheeled West on Fifth Street, stepping to a lively air. When in front of Segrud's Photo Gallery, the column halted and the entire instrumental aggregation filed inside to have pictures taken.

Then with an escort of 400 scholars from the Canton Public Schools, they marched down Bartlett, went east on Sixth Street, North on Broadway, east on Fifth Street, north on Lincoln, west on Fourth Street, south on Broadway, and west on Fifth Street to the Opera House. The sidewalks were lined with people and all admired the procession of handsome musicians in their bright uniforms, and enjoyed the peppy band music.

The afternoon program opened at the Opera House, which was jammed with admiring friends. It was a great day for Andrew. Seated before him were seventy-two band men. He stepped up to the podium. There simply was no experience equal to standing on a stage with hundreds of eyes staring at you, hundreds of ears listening, and realizing that for some endless minutes you were in charge of other people's emotions. He raised his baton and the concert began. The big sound of the four joint bands was pleasing to his ears. Why, he was conducting more band men than the great Sousa, who only had sixty musicians in his band.

There was a break in the music while John S. Erikson of Sioux Falls gave a talk on *The New Norway*, a subject everyone was interested in those days.

When the joint band finished their last concert number, and Andrew lowered his baton, the audience exploded in ovation. It was a magnificent concert.

But the day wasn't over. In the evening the singing groups – the *Grieg Sangforening* from Canton, and the *Minnehaha Mandskor* from Sioux Falls, together with the Wendt Orchestra took the stage. The evening concert pleased the packed Opera House audience. The sound of more than fifty men's voices as they sang in close harmony pleased Andrew also.

After the vocal and orchestra numbers, the audience demanded encores. Finally, the last selection was Andrew's own composition, *The Midnight Sun*, which was performed by the Wendt Orchestra. When it was finished, Andrew turned and bowed. The audience was now standing, and clapping. Bravos were echoing throughout the hall. This day had indeed been *Professor Indseth's Grand Musical Jubilee*! Andrew had been instructing some of those groups for fourteen years.

Business was booming in the fall of 1905. On Saturdays some of the stores were packed. Mr. Puckett said these were the busiest days he had ever had, and he decided to add thirty-five feet to the back of his store.

In November, John Anderson advertised in the *Dakota Farmer's Leader* that he had 500 pictures to give away at his furniture store on Saturday, November 13, and by 3:30 p.m. every picture was gone and people kept coming until 9 o'clock asking for pictures. Joe Anderson, the assistant to his father, said they could have handled 1500 pictures.

Young Martin Overseth, who played trumpet in the Moe Band, decided to join this active business climate in Canton, and on December 8, he bought out Silverburg's stock of goods, located in the Syndicate Block across from the Rudolph hotel. He advertised an elegant line of ladies skirts, first class line of overalls, shirts and dried goods. His 5, 10 and 15 cent counters were advertised as great money savers. He also carried a fine line of ladies hosiery, fresh groceries and canned goods.

Martin rented a room above the store where he and his brother Tony stayed. But there was a room in the back of the store that got to be a meeting place for musicians with their instruments. Several evenings a week, the men could be heard practicing. Often Ray and Andy and Joachim stopped in. Martin and Tony both were very interested and serious about their music – Martin with his trumpet and Tony with his trombone.

Andrew opened the letter he had just received. The postmark was from Sioux Falls. It read....

Dear Professor Indseth,

      On Monday, December 5th, the Minnehaha Mandskor of Sioux Falls will be celebrating their fifteenth anniversary. You were along and helped us organize in 1890, and we request your presence at our celebration. We would like to have you join us at a dinner in the hall in Sioux Falls on the evening of the 5th of December. The purpose of this event is to show our appreciation to those who helped us get started.

      Please let us know if you can attend.

The Minnehaha Mandskor

"Are you going?" Inger asked.

"Of course," was Andrew's quick reply. "I wonder how many of the singers who began way back then are still with them. I didn't have time to visit with many from the *Minnehaha Mandskor* at the Music Jubilee when they were here last month. It will be interesting to reminisce about those early days. I'll take the Cannon Ball (train). Now it makes two trips to Sioux Falls each day and returns.

"Fifteen years! Just think of how much time has passed since then." Andrew folded up the letter and then emphatically repeated, "*Of course I am going.*"

And it was a very nice event. Andrew was given a royal reception at the hands of the Sioux Falls singers and came home happy in the knowledge that the *Minnehaha Mandskor* was one of the strongest singing societies in the Northwest.

The editor of the *Dakota Farmer's Leader* who reported this news item, added...."*Professor Indseth has done more for music in this part of the state than any other man we know. He is also a composer of merit and a leader who has few equals.*"

Andrew Indseth Family - Circa 1907
Back row - Josephine, Malinda, Jennie, Roy, Florence and Inger Indseth
Front row: Inez, Berger, Andrew, Jr., Ray and A.K. Indseth

Chapter 17

*T*he family lingered around the breakfast table discussing the plans for the day. There was one fewer person at the table now as brother Joachim had moved to Decorah, Iowa, where he was involved in music and other opportunities.

The year of 1906 had already made its way into the month of March, a slow time on the farm.

"Are you going in to Canton tonight, Pa?" Andy asked his father.

"*Ja*, tonight is Grieg *Sangforening* practice. That's where I go on Tuesday nights."

"Is it alright if we ride along?"

Andy was referring to himself and his brothers Ray and Berger.

"Martin Overseth wants us to join him, his brother Tony, and a couple of other fellows in the back room of his store and play some fun music tonight."

"*Akkurat!*" was his father's answer. "Good for you boys! I only wish I could spend a relaxed evening just fooling around with musical instruments."

Andrew's sons could play almost any instrument, and they were proficient on all of them. This night in March, Andy took along his trombone, Ray brought his clarinet, and Berger, his cornet. Martin Overseth played cornet and Tony trombone. The boys had obtained music for some of the popular songs of the day, and when they got together they would play through some of them. A new piece they would be working on was...

> *"By the Sea, By the Sea, By the Beautiful Sea,*
> *You and Me, You and Me,*
> *Oh, how happy we will be."*

There was something satisfying and enjoyable about joining the various instrument sounds and making music.

The first of April, Martin Overseth decided to move his merchandise from his store in the Syndicate Block to the Gilbert Satrang building on Main Street. There was more shopping traffic on Main Street where most of the shops were. Martin had found that many customers didn't come over east by the Rudolph Hotel. This Satrang building also had a large back room, and at least once a week the boys would continue to get together; sometimes other band members would drop in too. All of these young men had music in their system.

However, the last of June, Martin was offered a good price for his stock of merchandise, and he closed his store. He took a traveling salesman job, and now he wasn't tied down with the store and had more time for music.

Andrew was extremely busy now. He had taken on more musical organizations – two men's choruses...the Inwood, Iowa, *Varde Mandskor*; the Beaver Creek, Minnesota, *Ulabrand Mandskor*; and the Moe orchestra.

Inger felt Andrew was getting too involved. Besides all the organizations he directed, he gave private vocal, piano, violin, and instrumental lessons. And it wasn't only the practices that he had to attend. Often these organizations and pupils would perform, and this brought Andrew to extra events. For instance, the Inwood Orchestra gave a concert at Alvord, Iowa, on a Saturday night and he had to attend that. The Moe Band often played in events in the Moe community. When his private pupils were asked to perform, they wanted him along to accompany them. At Luther League in Trinity Church, his vocal student, Gina Gubbrud, presented a sacred solo, and she had him accompany her. At the Canton High School Commencement, he joined Judith Sogn, a violin student, in a violin duet. Also at the Commencement, the Wendt Orchestra performed, which Andrew directed.

On Sunday, May 25, 1906, the newly rebuilt Trinity Church was dedicated. It was much finer and larger than the one the tornado of 1902 had destroyed. This structure faced the east. The beautiful pulpit, altar, and altar rail which the Satrum brothers had designed and crafted were in place. In the front of the church a colorful large religious painting had now been inserted in the altar, reaching upwards to the ceiling.

Besides the many speakers at the Dedication, music was supplied by choirs, soloists, and the new Moe Orchestra. Andrew was there to direct this orchestra. He had made simple arrangements of some hymns, which members of the new orchestra could master. When they played "*Oh Sacred Head Now Wounded*" with solo violin parts, it was especially worshipful. There was a great crowd in attendance.

In 1906, the Grieg Chorus was confused as to when to have their annual concert. The last few years it had been on May 17, celebrating Norway's Constitution Day, but now with the new independence in Norway, they decided to have it on June 7, the one-year anniversary of Norway's new independence. It was again held in the large assembly building at the Chautauqua grounds, and the program consisted of several prominent speakers, music by the Wendt Orchestra and the Grieg Chorus. All the Norwegian-Americans in the area were excited about the events in Norway and many were in attendance at the concert. It was a new era in the life of the old Northland country.

"*Andreas*, you have a letter from your brother, Hans, in Christiania. Maybe he is telling about the new King," Inger said, and she guessed right.

July 10, 1906
Dear Andreas and Inger,

 I know from the letter you sent that you are curious about the new situation here in Norway. We didn't become a republic as so many Norwegians in America suggested. But I feel we made the right decision.

 The new King and Queen were crowned in the stately Nidaros Cathedral in Trondhjem on June 22, which was two weeks ago. They arrived in Norway from Denmark in late 1905. Prince Karl changed his name to Haakon the VII, and his son's name to Olav. I feel that what Haakon the Good did for his people, it is possible for Haakon the VII to do.

 There has been much celebrating with concerts and special events here in Christiania and I have had the opportunity to see the new King Haakon and Queen Maude. Now we often hear the shouts of "Long live the King of Norway!" when he appears.

 I met our brother Joachim's son, Sigurd, in a shop the other day and had a short conversation with him. I understand that he and his mother and brother and sister had never planned to join Joachim in America. They are all well and getting along alright. I know you have been wondering about them.

 My family is fine. I have had some mass church choir concerts, and am busy as organist and also work with the school. It has been a long time since we have seen you, but understand all is going well with you and your family. I am very happy when I receive a letter from you,

 Your brother,
 Hans

After reading it, Andrew remarked, "I still think Norway should have changed to a republic!"

* * * * *

"Andy, Ray and Berger, when you finish your chores you must come in so we can start working on our concert pieces," father Andrew said. These practices would be held almost every day during June and until their July concert tour.

Andrew and his sons were booked to give several concerts in the Geddes, South Dakota area. They were advertised as *The Indseth Family Orchestra*. In lining up a program, Andrew made use of the boys' talents on both string and wind instruments. He arranged several special numbers combining duets, solos, and several quartets when he and the boys played together.

"You girls will have to do the chores when we are away," their father announced.

"You will have to milk the two cows, and see that all the animals have food and water."

"I'll see to it," Inger assured him.

Andrew and his sons left the Canton depot on Tuesday, July 20, for Geddes, to fill several dates in that county. They were gone four days, and had a very successful tour with good crowds and lots of encores. Andrew never said it out loud, but he was proud of his three boys.

Automobiles! Now they were catching on, and slowly, one by one, people were purchasing their own. After Martin Overseth sold out his store, he purchased an auto. He was always an immaculate dresser, but now when he arrived at a destination, he would often be dirty and even muddy, because the chain that turned the wheels would come off, and he would have to lie under the car on the dirt road to get it back in place.

From time to time, cars would drive up the Canton streets. Usually, the noisy autos would scare the horses, and those driving buggies dreaded meeting them on the narrow roads. As an example to show what often happened – a big red auto came into Canton from the west, and passed down Fifth Street at forty miles an hour. The horse of J. A. Carpenter that was tied in front of the telephone office became frightened, jumped, broke loose and ran away, leaving the buggy behind in a few jumps. It cost the driver ten dollars and costs. The speed limit in Canton was six miles an hour between crossings and four miles an hour over crossings.

The town of Beresford, South Dakota, was known as the car capital. There were sixteen autos in Beresford, and two more had been ordered. In July, during the Chautauqua, Canton became famous as an auto center because of the joys of a spin from Beresford over good roads and the splendid entertainment at the end of the trip. Often six or more autos from Beresford would rest in front of the Rudolph Hotel. As they came into Canton, the drivers would toot their tooters as if to say, "Look at us!" Usually the trip from Beresford was a ninety-minute ride.

* * * * *

Young people in the Moe community organized a big musical concert for September 23, 1906. It began at 1 p.m. and was held in the pasture at the farm of the newlyweds, John and Josie Engebretson, located two miles west of Moe. There was an admission charge at the gate: 10 cents for adults and children under twelve were free. Musical groups played all afternoon and evening – the Lincoln Fil Harmoni Orchestra, assisted by the Moe Orchestra and the Moe Band. The Dokken Male Quartet and Blandet Choir and a number of vocal soloists also took part. Because of the muddy roads, many could not attend, and it wasn't that enjoyable for those who were there to walk around in a pasture with muddy spots. Refreshments were served during the day and supper was served in the evening. Five hundred people attended in spite of the mud. Andrew had to be there to direct his Moe musical organizations.

This heavy rain had caused havoc at the Canton depot. The roof leaked so the telegraph operator had to cover his instruments, and the cashier's desk had to be covered to keep the records dry. Canton was in dire need of a new depot. Sometimes when delays occurred, there were one hundred passengers waiting, but there were no toilet rooms or other conveniences which women and children demanded.

In October, President Earling of the Milwaukee Railroad, came to Canton and inspected conditions at the depot, but his decision to only remodel the old depot greatly disappointed the Canton people. There still would be the absence of necessary modern conveniences.

* * * * *

Inger couldn't believe her eyes. The apple tree north of the house had blossoms, and it was September. She picked a few sprays to bring inside because there was no chance that they would make apples at this time of the year. She enjoyed their sweet fragrance in the house. Later, when she read the *Dakota Farmer's Leader*, she discovered that other people had apple trees blooming also. The editor stated that Lincoln County was the banana belt of South Dakota.

Business in Canton was very good. In October, O. H. Lybarger had a grand opening in his new Dollar Savings Store. He advertised men's overalls for fifty cents and work shirts for thirty-eight cents. He had previously had a shoe store in Canton.

Tom Sexe's Men's Store was busy. He promised that his fashion plates would make a young man look like a millionaire.

December second, the big bash at the Puckett-Pidcoe Grand Holiday Opening was a record-breaker. The musical program was fine and the coffee and cookies served were delicious. The handsome double-store had been remodeled after the thirty-five foot addition was added to the back of the store. The building was redecorated with ceilings in imitation moiré and walls in a handsome ingrain. Big overhead lights were in the back of each room, which shone light over the attractive surroundings.

And there were bargains in Canton: The Cash Shoe Store of the Bragstad Brothers advertised shoes –

> Little folks......................75cents to $1.00
> Small boys and girls.......$1.25 to $1.50
> Big boys and girls..........$1.50 to $1.75

In the grocery stores, apples could be purchased for 65 cents and 75 cents *per bushel.*

The Canton Augustana College was doing well too. Two hundred and fifty students had signed up for the winter term. President Tuve needed accommodations for one hundred students and he advertised for rooms in Canton homes.

Chapter 18

"There was a fire at the depot last night," Andrew reported. He had just returned from a trip into Canton. "Quite a bit of damage. It started in the baggage room, and before the fire could be extinguished, the east end of the depot was almost destroyed. I wonder now if the Milwaukee will try to fix it, or if they will give us a new one." Andrew fingered his whiskers and then added, "I guess we'll just have to wait and see."

It had been a cold January day, and when Andrew sat down at the kitchen table, Inger poured him a cup of hot coffee and set the sugar bowl on the table. She joined him with her cup.

Inger changed the subject. "How were the sidewalks in town today?"

The City Council in November of 1906 had made a new law. The sidewalks on Main Street had become so filthy from tobacco-chewers spitting on them that the Council finally decided it was time to do something about it. On the first of January, 1907, "*No Spitting*" signs had gone up all over town, and the result for disobeying them would be fines of five dollars, up to twenty-five dollars. The Council figured that the only way to stop this was to have the offenders feel it in their pocketbooks. Five dollars was a lot of money in those days.

Andrew's answer to her question was, "I couldn't see much improvement today.

"When I came out of the post office, there were two men standing there. The one man spit a big wad right on the sidewalk. The other fellow told him, 'It's a good thing the Marshal didn't see you, or you would have to pay.' When they looked up the street, there, only a half block away, was the Marshal and he was headed in their direction. You should have seen how fast that man stepped on his mess with both of his big feet. When the Marshal came by, this man was busily reading his mail, and he did not look up nor budge from the spot. If this scare didn't teach him a lesson today, then I'm afraid one of these days he'll get caught and have to pay."

Inger said, "I'll have to write Inez and tell her about the new law. Last year, she was really upset that no one was doing anything about the unsanitary sidewalks."

The *Grieg Sangforening* held their annual election at the Grieg Hall the last of January, 1907. The new officers were Charles O. Knudson, President; P.A. Sorum, Vice President; G. G. Sorum, Secretary; H. Greguson, corresponding secretary; A. N. Bragstad, Treasurer; Ed Isakson, Marshal; T. T. Sexe, H. F. Quien, Ed Graneng, banner carriers; H. Greguson, P.A. Sorum, and Hans Graneng, music committee; Prof. Indseth, instructor, and G. S. Hansen, assistant instructor. There had been some changes in the membership of the *Grieg Mandskor* through the years. New members had been added, and some had moved away or retired, but still there was a basic core of the charter members.

At the meeting, the question came up as to when their 1907 annual concert should be held. Last year it had been June 7, the one-year anniversary of Norway's new independence. The members had noticed that many other organizations had continued celebrating on May 17.

One of the members spoke up, "June 7 worked out very well last year. If we have a picnic along with it, the weather is nicer in June. After all, it will be the second anniversary of Norway's new freedom. The assembly building on the Chautauqua grounds gives us a lot of room. We do have large crowds."

Andrew had this suggestion: "I have an idea for a little different program this year. I have been directing two other *Mandskors* (men's choruses) in the area - the *Varde*, from Inwood, Iowa, and the *Ulabrand*, from Beaver Creek, Minnesota. They, of course, are also Norwegian, and would approve of celebrating Norway's Independence with us.

"If we put the men's voices from all three choruses together, it will be a splendid sound. It would make a good program, along with the Wendt Orchestra as usual."

This was agreed upon, and Andrew told them, "When we choose the music, I'll get all three choruses working on the same numbers. We have many months to work on them so I feel we can have a very outstanding program."

Several weeks later, the members of the Grieg Chorus and their ladies surprised President Knudson at his home on a Wednesday evening. The Grieg fellows often honored their new presidents with a special social event. There was an abundance of good music and good fellowship. The ladies had taken along a generous supply of eatables, and a delicious lunch was served. Superintendent C. G. Lawrence, on behalf of the Chorus, then presented Mr. and Mrs. Knudson each with a fine rocking chair. The gathering was a most happy one for all concerned.

At the breakfast table on the last Sunday in March, 1907, Andrew informed his family, "I can't go along to church today." He explained, "The *Varde Mandskor* of Inwood, Iowa, is coming to Canton on the noon train and they are having a group picture taken at A. T. Segrud's Gallery. As their director, they want me along in the picture. They have it set for immediately after they arrive, and most of them plan to return home on the 2 o'clock train."

"How many members does this new *Mandskor* have?" Inger asked.

"About the same as the Grieg – twenty-two members," was Andrew's reply.

"They couldn't get another time worked out when all the men could be available, and when the train schedule worked for them. I have no choice. I must be there."

* * * * *

The month of April began a session in Andrew's life that he would like to forget. It started with a splitting headache, and then a high fever. Finally, Inger called the doctor, who came out and checked him. At first the doctor wasn't sure what was ailing Andrew, but the next day when his fever had risen to 104 degrees, and a rash appeared, he announced, "I am afraid that Andrew has small pox. I will have to quarantine all of you."

Inger had been vaccinated as a child, so the doctor gave her instructions for Andrew's care. "Inger, you must keep putting cold cloths on his head and body around the clock to try to get the temperature down. Andrew is a very sick man. We must get the fever down or he may go into delirium."

The doctor then turned to the rest of the family, "We must quickly do something about the rest of you. You all will be quarantined because we don't know if you have been infected. Small pox is one of the most contagious of infectious diseases and we don't want any of you, nor any other people to get it. Tomorrow I will come out and get you vaccinated. The incubation period is from seven to seventeen days, so you all will have to watch for symptoms and let me know."

Inger was fearful for her family. If her children kept in contact with Andrew now and through the next weeks they could become infected. She had an idea.

"I think you children should move out to the shanty. There's a stove out there where I heat the water when I do the laundry. The sooner you get out of the house, the safer. Take quilts and the clothes you will need - not dressy things because you won't be going any place. And, Jenny, you girls take a few kettles along so you can make meals for everyone."

This shanty had been the first home on this farm. It consisted of one large room, with a loft. It had not been demolished after the new house was built, and it was used for laundry and for cooking in the summer so as to not heat up the big house.

Inger became very busy nursing Andrew day and night. Every hour found her at the kitchen sink pumping cold water for the cloths for Andrew's head and body. On the fourth day, the fever broke and blisters began to appear. The doctor provided medicine for the itching.

Every day Jenny or Ray or Andy talked to their mother through the screen door. The children were concerned about their father, and Inger was anxious to hear if any of them were getting sick. Inger ordered groceries using the telephone, and these were delivered and set on the porch where Jennie could pick up what she needed.

"Jennie, I'll depend on you to carefully watch everyone. If anyone gets a headache or fever, let me know so we can get the doctor."

The small pox illness proceeded in its usual pattern. However, the doctor told Inger, "We are lucky that Andrew didn't get a hard case of it." After the lesions dried up, the quarantine sign was taken down, and Andrew gradually got his strength back, but Inger was all worn out. With the girls back in the house again to help her, Inger tried to get some rest. She began taking a nap in the afternoon, which became a habit that she continued the rest of her life.

On May 4, 1907, Andrew went into Canton to take care of some business. He met and visited with the editor, and this is what the editor printed in the newspaper:

> Professor A. K Indseth, who has been having a tussle with small pox, has recovered, and is once more able to be out. He did not enjoy being shut up, but was very happy to know that none of the other members of his family took the disease.

*   *   *   *   *

After being laid up for a month, Andrew tried to make up for the time he had lost. He had to get the three men's choruses ready for the June 7 concert.

Also, May 22, the Grieg Chorus was to present a musical selection at the laying of the cornerstone of the large new Canton Lutheran Church which was now being built. On that Sunday afternoon a large crowd gathered at the site. It was an exciting day for members of the joint Lutheran church. The building had begun, with John Millie preparing the foundation. Music was also presented by the church choir and the Augustana College choir.

Rev. Nummedal from Moe gave a short message at the cornerstone laying, which was very meaningful to the group gathered there.

"The real Church is not a building," he reminded them. "It is God's people. Jesus is the Cornerstone, and we are the living stones that make up His invisible Church." He closed with, "May God bless this new building as He meets you in it."

Andrew and Inger attended the closing festivities of the day - a sacred concert in the evening in the old twin churches. Professor Olai Seeberg was at the organ, and his wife, a soprano soloist, joined him. The audience greatly enjoyed the pipe organ music and vocal numbers.

The twin churches were now to be dismantled. Services were to be held in the Augustana College Chapel during the summer, and it was hoped that the church would be completed sufficiently by fall to provide a meeting place in the basement during the winter.

* * * * * *

The second anniversary of Norway's Independence Day was celebrated in Canton on Friday, June 7, 1907, under the auspices of the *Grieg Sangforening* at the Chautauqua park. It began at 1 p.m.

> Music........Luther League Band
> Selection.............Wendt Orchestra
> "*Ja, Vi Elsker Dette Landet*"...Ulabrand, Varde and Grieg Choruses
> "*Naturen Och Hjerat*".........Grieg Sangforening
> "*Jeg Vil Verge Mit Land*".......Ulabrand, Varde and Grieg Choruses
> America.................Ulabrand, Varde and Grieg Choruses
> "*Saeterjenten's Sondag*" (Chalet Girl's Sunday) , baritone solo...
>   P.A.Sorum and the Grieg Sangforening
> "*Fanevagt*"..........Ulabrand, Varde and Grieg Choruses
> "*Offa Fjerderne Graa*" and "*Danda Raabte Fellen*"...Grieg
>   Sangforening
> "*Norge, Norge*"..............Grieg Sangforening
>   Admission – 25 cents   Children under 15 – free

Sixty-five men's voices in close harmony, sometimes singing a cappella, was a sound that was pleasing to the audience, even to those who couldn't understand Norwegian, and it was pleasing to Andrew. This was the sound he had been striving for. And the people with Norwegian blood running in their veins all joined in celebrating Norway's new Independence Day.

After the June seventh concert, where he played in the Wendt Orchestra, Andy, Jr. packed some clothes, and his trombone, and boarded the train, heading for Slayton, Minnesota, where he would play in a summer resort orchestra.

Two members of the Moe Band also left for the summer. On May 24, Martin Overseth joined his brother in Grand Island, Nebraska, where Anton had been attending business college. The two young men then went on to Abilene, Kansas to join the Parker Carnival. They had signed up with the carnival band for the summer as it toured across the country to the west coast.

* * * * *

September 4, 1907, was a sad day in the musical world. The Great E*dvard Grieg* passed away in Bergen, Norway, of heart failure. He was Norway's famous composer and pianist. His music had the distinct sound of his native land – Norway, but he was respected and honored worldwide. Now he was gone, but he had left behind a quantity of beautiful music, which would be enjoyed for centuries to come.

John Philip Sousa and his band were in Mitchell again in 1907. Special trains were running September 23 through September 28. Andrew and his boys and many other musicians from the Canton area attended, but this time they sat in the audience.

In the fall the Indseth family moved back into the town of Canton. Halvor Martin, their landlord, had sold his land and the new owners were taking over. Andrew found a house on the south edge of town. This pleased Inger, who liked to be able to view the countryside.

In December, Andrew and his boys began working on the program they would present on their next tour, which was lined up for January, 1908. *The Indseth Family Orchestra was going* on the road again.

Boating on Sioux River at Chautauqua Park
Canton, South Dakota

Professor Inseth and his Fairvew Band - Circa 1910

Professor Indseth, in the center of the 3rd row, with baton

First row - Roy Indseth with flute (2nd from left) Second row - Anton Bekke with clarinet (1st on left),
Hans Bekke with clarinet (3rd from left), Martin Overseth with cornet (6th from left)
Back row - Andrew Indseth Jr. with baritone (3rd from left), Tony Overseth with trombone (4th from left)

Chapter 19

*I*n January of 1908, the *The Indseth Family Orchestra* loaded their musical instruments on the train at Canton to begin their concert tour. Andy came with his cello, trombone and violin, Ray with his clarinet, cornet and violin, and Berger with his violin, cornet, and drum. Father Andrew had his violin and cornet. The family had been practicing and preparing for this for many weeks, and now the excitement of the tour had set in. They were on their way.

The Professor had worked up some fun numbers along with some classical music. After seeing the popular response to brother Joachim's humorous piece in Hudson, Andrew decided to put variety in the program. He wanted to please his audiences.

On Friday, January 28, at the end of their tour, Andrew and his boys gave their program at Fairview, South Dakota. It was a grand success and the Fairview Hall was packed to hear the Professor and his three sons, who were all able musicians.

The Professor sang a Norwegian solo,"*Den Gang da Var Pige*" (Once there was a Girl), in a humorous manner, to the accompaniment of two violins and a cello. After a hearty encore, Professor Indseth put in a second appearance and sang, "*Den Gang da Jeg Var Gutt*" (Once when I was a Boy).

Berger was the star of the next number. He was blackened and was dressed in a worn rolled-up pants and a bright shirt and sang to a violin and shoe-heel accompaniment. He made quite a splash on stage with his jig as he sang "*Oh! Oh! Miss Lucy Ella*".

The string quartet pieces with father and three sons on three violins and a cello, and with all four violins were splendid. And so were the brass quartet numbers. The crowd enjoyed the concert very much.

The village of Fairview was nestled between the hills on the South Dakota - Iowa border. It was situated along a bend in the Sioux River, halfway between Canton and Hudson. Many Norwegian immigrants had settled in this area because this spot with its hills reminded them of Norway. The Milwaukee Railroad ran through the village, which made Sioux City, Sioux Falls, and Canton easily accessible.

On February 14, 1908, the village of Fairview received two new residents, Martin and Tony Overseth. A deal had been completed whereby Martin and Anton Overseth became owners of *Erickson Hardware Store* in Fairview, which now became known as the *Overseth Brothers Hardware*. The boys had traded some land they owned in Hand County to Mr. Erickson for his hardware store. Martin and Tony had returned to Canton the previous fall after their stint with the Parker Carnival band that had brought them to California. Now Martin was back as proprietor of a store again.

Tony and Martin, now living in Fairview, missed the musical camaraderie they had had in Canton, but they soon discovered that many men and young boys were interested in starting a band in Fairview. They contacted Andrew and talked him into instructing and directing them.

Lots of snow, and even blizzards descended on southeastern South Dakota the first three months of 1908. At times even the trains were snowbound. One night in the middle of March it began to rain, but by morning another eight inches of wet snow had accumulated. When all of the snow began to melt, the Sioux River went on a rampage. Huge ice chunks blocked the flow of the river and made ice jams under the railroad bridge near Canton so the railroad men had to dynamite them. Again, the end of May, the river rose eight feet, the highest mark since 1881, but, thankfully, it began to go down the next day. All of this water flooded the Chautauqua grounds which were located along the river and much clean-up and sunshine was needed to get it ready for Chautauqua time in July.

* * * * *

"Inger, are you ready?" Andrew called to his wife. Tonight she was dressed in her long sleeved white blouse with all the tiny tucks and lace, and her long black skirt. At the neck of the blouse was a pin she had brought along from Norway. Inger put on her black straw Sunday hat with the big silk flower on it and headed for the kitchen door. Tonight was a special night. The *Grieg Sangforening* was having a social in Andrew's honor.

On June 12, 1858, Andreas Kristian Indseth had been born in Kristiansund, Norway, and now, June 12, 1908, in Canton, South Dakota, USA, it was time to celebrate his 50th birthday. The celebration was to be held in the Grieg Hall, and all of the wives of the *Grieg Sangforening* members were included. There was a big birthday cake and other delicious foods, and there was singing and speeches. Many of the members expressed their appreciation of Andrew's leadership and the excellent musical instruction he had given them, and they all showered him with good wishes.

*   *   *   *   *   *

The fire in the Canton depot in 1907 had changed the minds of the Milwaukee Railroad people, and in the fall of 1907, they began to build a *new* depot in Canton. By August, 1908, it was completed, and it occupied an entire block. It had been built two blocks west of the old depot because the necessary land needed couldn't be purchased in the old location. This depot had accommodations for the ladies with a waiting room at the west end, and the gentlemen's smoking room was separated from the ladies by the ticket office and telegraph room. East of the smoking room was the lunch room, and a large roofed pavilion with a brick floor connected the baggage and express rooms with the main building. There was hot water heat and electricity. The Canton people thought it was the finest depot in the state. Andrew used the train a couple of times a week, traveling to his practices at Inwood and now Fairview, and he appreciated the new depot.

On Saturday evening, December 5, 1908, the newly organized Fairview Band gave its first concert in the Fairview Hall. Martin and Tony had persuaded Andy, Ray and Berger to join the band. A fine program was rendered, consisting of band and orchestra music, reading and singing. The young people who attended the concert reported a fine time. With Professor Indseth as instructor, the Fairview Band boys were doing splendid work, and everyone enjoyed the concert.

The interest in the Fairview band increased. In April of 1909, some of the talented Moe Band members – Louie and Gust Dokken and Anton Bekke, who were friends of Martin and Tony, decided to join the Fairview bunch. By the end of April a portable bandstand had been built, in which the first concert was held on Saturday, May the eighth.

On May 17, 1909, the village of Fairview celebrated the Norwegian holiday. The band played all day, and there were races, kicking contests, and a ball game.

The Fairview Band was a very active band. At first, the boys gave band concerts every Saturday night on the streets of Fairview, but when summer came, they played both Wednesday and Saturday nights.

This arrangement worked out fine for Tony and Martin Overseth, who lived in an apartment above their Hardware Store. They were always ready to make music.

In August, the Moe Debate Club held a picnic in the Paul Thompson Gubrud grove two miles east of Moe. They had invited the Fairview Band, under the direction of Professor Indseth, to present a little concert, and the Band responded with many audience-pleasing numbers.

Two of the Debate Club members, P.S. Paulson and Adolph Gubrud, gave speeches. The Trinity Ladies Aid served lunch, and the Debate Club had a stand of lemonade, fruit and candy. There were races and kicking contests too.

The first of December, 1909, the large new red granite Canton Lutheran Church was finished. A date had been chosen for the dedication, but the date was changed because some of the chairs and some of the parts for the new organ hadn't arrived. Finally on Christmas Day, at the 10:30 a.m. service, Rev. Tetlie gave his first sermon in the new church building and the congregation got to hear the new organ for the first time.

The week before Christmas, Inger and the girls – Josie, Florence and Millie (Malinda), made a shopping trip into Canton. They were buying gifts for Christmas and the necessary supplies for the *Julekveld* (Christmas Eve) supper. Andrew had already picked up a Christmas tree.

Pappa, you can't imagine the crowds in Canton today," Josie reported when they returned home.

Millie explained, "We even had to wait to get into Lybarger's Dollar Store. He had to close the doors for an hour because the crowd was so large inside."

"Did you get the *lutefisk*?" Andrew asked.

"Yes," Inger said, "and Hanson and Grevlos had lingonberries today too."

The girls went to their bedrooms with their purchases and Inger poured up coffee for Andrew and herself, and then sat down at the kitchen table with her husband.

"The next thing I have to do now is the Christmas baking – the *lefse, flat-brød, fattigmand, krumkake*, and doughnuts, and maybe some *berlinerkrand-ser*. Everyone likes that."

Inger took a sip of the hot coffee, was thoughtful for a moment, and then said to Andrew, "I'll miss Jennie this year. She was always so good to help me with the *lefse*."

"*Ja*, Jennie's trip to visit her sister in North Dakota this summer has gotten pretty lengthy," Andrew noted. "Now that she found a job up there, it'll probably be a while before we see her again."

"I imagine Jennie and Inez will be baking *lefse* and Christmas cookies up in North Dakota this year," Inger surmised.

"The rest of the family will be together Christmas Eve," Inger reminded her husband. "I'm thankful for that. I believe Christmas Eve is a special time for each of them."

And then she added, "And for me too! Especially after we've eaten and when we sing the Christmas songs together. We all are so happy when we sing "*Jeg er Saa Glad Vaer Julekveld*", and when we sing "*Glade Jul*" (Silent Night) in parts, without an accompaniment, it is so special.

"As we quietly and reverently sing that song, it is like a hush falls over us - kind of like a benediction. *That is Christmas for me!*"

Chapter 20

The new year of 1910 began for Andrew and his sons on New Year's Eve as they and the two Overseth boys played for a social dance at the Woodman's Hall in Fairview. It was advertised as "*music by the Indseth-Overseth Orchestra*", and included Andrew, Ray, Andy, Jr., Berger and Martin and Tony Overseth. They were booked by a group from the Fairview area, and the report in the newspaper stated "*a pleasant time was enjoyed by all.*"

This happened to be the last time that Andrew and all of his sons would perform together because the following week Ray surprised his parents with this statement: "I've decided to move to Omaha. My twenty-sixth birthday is coming up in a few months and it's time for me to get out on my own."

He glanced from his mother to his father to see how they were taking his news, and then he added, "I'm thinking of going to a big city where there are a variety of jobs to be had."

"Couldn't you just go to Sioux Falls?' his father asked.

"No, Pa, I plan to move to Omaha."

Andrew was quiet for a few minutes as he considered what this would mean, not only for Ray, but for him and the rest of the family. So he then asked, "Have you thought this over, Ray? What about *our* music?"

"Yes, Pa, I've thought this over. I can't make a living playing my instruments in these small towns. I want to get out in the world and make some money."

"Are you planning to leave soon?"

"Maybe in a couple of weeks," he informed them.

So several weeks later, Ray packed his suitcase, took his clarinet and violin, said goodbye to his parents, and boarded the train for Omaha.

Professor Andrew Indseth was now minus one member of his family orchestra.

Every year after the Christmas holidays there always seemed to come a round of illnesses to the community – colds and grippe. This year it made the rounds in the Indseth family with coughing, fever and chills. Andrew and the rest of the family were soon back at their busy schedules again, but Berger couldn't seem to snap out of it. He was up and around, but he couldn't shake his cough, and he was so tired all the time. His doctor said he didn't know anything else to do for him, except perhaps he should get away. His doctor knew of a doctor in Denver, Colorado, who specialized in getting patients back to good health when they were run down. Perhaps Berger should check into that. In the meantime, his mother saw to it that he kept warm and got plenty of rest; and she coaxed him to eat by preparing his favorite foods.

By the first of May, Berger still wasn't in good health, so he took his doctor's suggestion and headed for Denver, Colorado. After four weeks there his health had returned, and he felt the trip had helped him greatly. Upon reaching Canton on May 27, the first place he went was to Lennox where a special lady, Lela Everson, lived with her parents.

Meanwhile, the Fairview Band was busy presenting concerts. With neither Ray nor Berger along now, Andrew was using other members of his family. On March 5, 1910, the Fairview Band played at the Opera House in Hudson. The program was composed largely of band music, interspersed with vocal and musical solos and duets.

The piano solo by Miss Esther Pond was certainly fine. She was a splendid musician for a young lady of her age, and her accompaniments were perfect.

Her brother, Lowell, a lad of ten or so, played a very fine cornet solo. A younger brother, Donald, was the snare drummer in the band.

Martin and Anton Overseth were so heartily encored when they played their cornet and trombone duet that they had to respond to the encore.

Then Andrew had two of his daughters, Misses Florence and Josie, sing a vocal duet, which was enjoyed by all.

Miss Alpha Hanson was ill and could not fill her part of the program so Andrew in the last minute coached his youngest son, Master Roy, who was only 11 years old. Roy sang the solo she was supposed to sing, "*I'd Love to Live in Loveland with a Girl Like You*," which was a hit with the audience.

After the concert, a dance was given. The orchestra was comprised of members of the band. Andrew's daughter, Florence, a violinist, was also part of the orchestra.

The editor of the *Hudsonite* wrote the following -

Professor A. K. Indseth is certainly a band leader without a
peer and he has done wonders with the band from our sister city to
the north, but he has some mighty good material to work with, for
there are some natural-born musicians among the 22 members of
that band.

The Hudson people were certainly well pleased with the concert
and the Fairview Band will be welcomed here, whenever they decide to favor us with another visitation.

On Sunday afternoon, May 13, the members of the Fairview Band went up
to Canton on the train to have their picture taken in their fine new uniforms at
A. T. Segrud's Studio. Andrew, with his baton, Andy with his trombone, and
young Roy with his flute, joined them there and were also in the picture.

Afterwards, the boys paraded over to the Rudolph Hotel, where out in
front they rendered a number of selections to serenade the friendly landlord
of the Rudolph. The popular Colonel T. J. McDermott had the reputation of
setting the best table and running the cleanest all around hotel in the state. He
had nineteen people working for him. McDermott was known to all as a jolly
good fellow.

On February 14, 1910, Andrew joined the other Grieg members, as the
Grieg Sangforening held their seventeenth annual meeting. Charles O. Knud-
son was again elected President; C. G. Lawrence, Vice President; Joe Chraft,
Secretary; Ed Graneng, Treasurer; G. G. Satrum, corresponding Secretary.
The Secretary and Treasurer reports were read, after which the men spent some
time rehearsing.

At the conclusion, a social time was enjoyed with a fine lunch provided
by Charles Knudson and G. S. Hanson. A number of speeches were given by
members. President Knudson acted as toastmaster. The editor of the *Sioux
Valley News* in his write-up, reported...

"This well-known musical society of our city was found to be in a
most prosperous condition, and has a membership of twenty-four."

* * * * * *

With the new pipe organ in the Canton church, the Luther League spon-
sored an organ recital as a fundraiser, on the twenty-eighth of January. They
secured Professor H. H. Hunt of Minneapolis, who was assisted by soloist
Stella Sogn, who lived in the Beloit, Iowa, area south of Canton. This was one
of the first opportunities for many to hear this new pipe organ. Andrew, with
his organ training, was interested and attended this excellent program.

Professor Hunt selected a variety of pieces to display the tone and power of the new organ –

> *1. Processional – Dubois*
> *2. Romance – Harress*
> *3. Solo – Stella Sogn*
> *4. Largo – Handel*
> *5. Spring Song – Hollins*
> *6. To a Wild Rose – Mac Dowell*
> *7. The Answer – Wolstenholme*
> *8. At Evening – Buck*
> *9. Selected Hymns and Chorals*
> *10. Album Leaf - Grieg*
> *11. Noel – Giulmant*
> *12. Holy Night – Buck*
> *13. Andantino – Lemare*
> *14. Marche Solennelle – Lemaegre*

After the concert, it was the consensus that this instrument proved to be worthy to fill a space in the handsome new edifice.

June 3, 1910, was the day of the new Canton Lutheran Church dedication. It was a great event in Canton. At the Sunday morning service, Professor F. Melius Christiansen, from St. Olaf College, presided at the new pipe organ. Dinner was served in the basement to more than one thousand people.

The next evening, Monday, June 4, an audience of one thousand was at the church to enjoy a concert by this prominent St. Olaf musician and organist, Professor F. Melius Christiansen, and Madame Marta Sandal-Bramsen, soprano. Christiansen was a master of the pipe organ, and his group of selections that night were well-arranged, and most pleasantly rendered. The program was a long one, but it was thoroughly enjoyed by a large audience, which included Andrew and Inger. Andrew had great respect for Professor Christiansen, and his musical abilities. He had heard about Christiansen's success leading the St. Olaf Band. Eventually Christiansen would become a well known director of the St. Olaf Choir.

In 1909 the Canton Band which Andrew had previously directed, had disbanded, but the Canton community and business men were anxious to have a band available for community events, so they were trying to get another one started. They even had a bandstand built for a band. The following notice appeared in the March fourth *Sioux Valley News*.......

"All who played in the band last summer, and any who may wish to join the band, are requested to meet at the Banquet Hall next Monday at 8 p.m. for the first practice. We hope boys will meet with the encouragement and support of the business men.

- Peter Anderson, leader.

*   *   *   *   *

Andrew and Inger's son, Berger, had become engaged, and with a marriage coming up, Berger was looking for a way to make a living. He had helped in a barber shop in Canton before, and he decided that this was what he wanted to do. He would open up his own barber shop.

"A barber shop is just what we need here in Fairview," Martin and Tony Overseth kept telling him. So Berger joined the business men in Fairview and opened his shop there the first week in July, 1910. Another plus for Martin and Tony, was that now they would have Berger back in the Fairview Band.

Andrew was spending a considerable amount of time in Fairview now. He had started a Singing School there in April. This was a new concept which many Norwegian Lutheran communities were trying. It was mainly to train young people to learn to sing. Here they were taught to read notes and sing in parts. Sopranos, altos, tenors, and basses would learn the parts of the song separately, and when they were familiar with their part, the teacher would combine them all. This training greatly improved the singing in the church choirs.

Now, since Berger had a barber shop in Fairview, Andrew often stopped to visit with the men sitting there. He was proud of his son, who was always so friendly, patient and kind to his customers and to the visitors that assembled there every day.

All the trips to Fairview for the band concerts Wednesday and Saturday nights in the summer, the Singing School and weekly band practices, and now with Berger living there, prompted Andrew to begin looking for a place in Fairview where his family could live.

*   *   *   *   *

In June, Andrew and the members of the *Grieg Sangforening* were putting in extra practice preparatory to going to the big *Northwestern Sangerfest* at Sioux Falls which was coming up the middle of July, 1910. The 10th biennial *Northwestern Norwegian-Danish Singers Association* would hold their great *Sangerfest* July 15, 16 and 17.

The *Sangerfest* was comprised of thirty-five singing groups from Illinois, Iowa, Wisconsin, Minnesota, and North and South Dakota. An estimated six hundred male voices would present concerts at the auditorium in Sioux Falls on Friday and Saturday evenings.

The members of the *Grieg Sangforening* of Canton would be participating in the program, as would Andrew's two other choruses – the *Varde Mandskor* of Inwood, Iowa, and the *Ulabrand Mandskor* of Beaver Creek, Minnesota. An orchestra of thirty instruments would be playing, and each day three bands would be on the streets entertaining the visitors and helping keep up enthusiasm. On Friday, Andrew was busy juggling his time between the *Sangerfest* activities and his Fairview band, who were playing on the Sioux Falls streets that day.

The Canton *Grieg Sangforening* made a striking appearance in the *Sangerfest Parade* with red, white, and blue umbrellas with their name in plain letters.

The concerts were not as well attended as expected, but they were very pleasing.

Chapter 21

"**Y**ou'll like it down by Fairview," Andrew promised Inger. "The hills around the little town will remind you of Norway. It's a pretty, peaceful place."

The Indseth family was moving again. At least, part of them. Andrew had found a house near Fairview, but only Andy, Florence and young Roy were moving with their parents. Milly (Malinda) and Josie were going to Sioux Falls where they had found work, and of course, Berger had his apartment in the back of his barber shop in Fairview.

The Indseths had just arrived when the little town of Fairview had visitors. Covered wagons came through town and gypsy women were stopping people and wanting to tell everyone's fortunes. However, they soon left town because they couldn't find Fairview residents who were interested.

After getting settled, Inger and Andrew received a letter from North Dakota from their daughter Jennie -

October 7, 1910
Dear folks,
> **I'm taking two weeks off from my job and am going to catch the train for Sioux Falls and visit you and my brothers and sisters in South Dakota.**
> **I'll be around there for almost two weeks.**
> > **Love,**
> > **Jennie**

First, Jennie stopped in Sioux Falls and got in touch with Millie and Josie.

"I'll go along down to Fairview with you," sister Josie said.

The two girls were pleased with their parents' home near Fairview. "I'll have to describe it to Inez when I get back," Jenny told them.

They checked out brother Berger's barber shop, and while they were in Fairview, Berger had his fiancée, Lela Everson, from Lennox come down so she could be introduced to all of the family. Berger was so proud of her. Berger and Lela had set the date for their wedding for Wednesday, December 14.

"Can you come, Jennie?" Berger asked her.

"After being here now, I don't believe I can make it; although I certainly would like to."

Jennie had some news of her own. She was getting married also. It would take place up in North Dakota at Inez's home. She was changing her name to Poe.

"I wouldn't be surprised if our sister Milly will soon change her name to Thallas." Josie informed them. "She has this friend up in Sioux Falls."

Andrew gave a little laugh as he said, "It looks like the wedding bug has been busy."

In the fall of 1910, the *Grieg Sangforening* started out their new season with five new members. They made arrangements for a concert to be given at the Canton Lutheran Church on Thanksgiving night. It would be a fund-raiser for the Canton Lutheran organ fund.

Besides the selections by the men's voices, they would be assisted by Mrs. Frank Anderson, Webster, South Dakota, soprano; Miss Ora Johnson, organist of the North Avenue Church, Chicago; and Miss Inez Johnson, elocutionist, a graduate of the American Conservatory of Chicago.

Andrew soon had his men practicing the music he had chosen. The Grieg Chorus always drew a good crowd.

*   *   *   *   *

On December 14, the entire Indseth family headed for Lennox.

Martin and Tony Overseth had been invited to Berger's wedding also. Martin and Tony each had automobiles now. Tony had purchased an Overland in Sioux Falls in June, and Martin was driving his second automobile.

The wedding took place at Lela's parents' home in Lennox – Mr. and Mrs. Nels Everson's.

"We'll give you and your folks a ride if you like," the Overseth boys had told Andy. "Then your family won't need to take the train."

It was a happy groom and a pretty bride who were married by Rev. Herbert of the Lennox Methodist Church. The radiant couple was showered with well wishes by family and guests. Now the new bride would be moving into Berger's little apartment in the back of his barber shop.

134

*   *   *   *   *   *

Inger and Andrew received a Christmas card from their son Ray in Omaha. He had written.......

"I'm sorry I can't make it for Christmas. With the job I have, the holidays are the busy season. I'll be thinking of you on Christmas Eve.

Love,

Ray

P.S. I will miss Mother's lefse."

Inger began preparing for Christmas – baking cookies, *flatbrød, lefse*, and *Julekake* (Christmas bread). She had been informed that Berger and his bride would be with them Christmas Eve and would spend Christmas Day with her parents.

On Christmas Eve, Millie and Josie arrived from Sioux Falls, and Berger and Lela came over from their apartment. They joined Andy, Florence and young Roy. As the family members gathered, there was always that special Christmas excitement in the air.

While the girls helped their mother in the kitchen, the men and Berger and his bride visited in the living room.

Christmas is often a time for memories, and father Andrew jogged Berger's memory with this question, "Do you remember the year you thought there would be no Christmas?"

"Yes," Berger said. "I was really worried."

Berger then explained to his bride that it was the year baby Josie was born, and he was only six years old, "but it turned out to be a good Christmas after all." he added.

"Pa, do you remember you told Milly and me to look for the *Julestjerne* (Christmas star)?"

"*Ja,*, and I remember that we found it!"

Berger took his bride over to the big window and suggested, "Let's see if it is shining tonight." As they looked up into the dark sky, there were many stars twinkling.

"Is that it?" Lela asked, as she pointed to the brightest one.

"It doesn't seem as bright as the one we saw when I was six years old," Berger said, " but it could be." Then he added, "Pa said it probably was the star that led the Wise Men to the baby Jesus. Who knows?"

The *Julekveld* meal was ready. Inger called them to the table. There were *lutefisk, lefse*, potatoes, and the trimmings, and lots of Christmas cookies.

Afterwards, it was time to sing and read the Christmas Gospel. Tonight Andrew got his violin and played variations on the Christmas carols. When Andrew and his violin made music, it came out with feeling and expressed the Christmas joy.

Then it was time to sing "*Jeg er Saa Glad Vaer Julekveld*", and all the family happily joined in song. Finally, without an accompaniment, Andrew led his family in "*Glade Jul*" (Silent Night), and it was beautifully sung in the usual quiet holy manner. Again this Christmas *hush* descended on them.

"*That was so special!*" Lela exclaimed.

Inger and everyone else agreed that this was what Christmas was all about.

Chapter 22

The old year of 1910 had gone out like a lamb, but 1911 came in like a lion on the warpath, which pleased the coal dealers and clothing men.

After Christmas, the annual round of sicknesses began. This year the grippe seemed to be a more serious type of influenza. Many who contacted it had it develop into pneumonia. It seemed to be contagious. Among others, two of Rev. Nummedal's daughters had serious bouts with pneumonia. Little Opal was very sick, and Sarah, who was attending Augustana College, also came down with pneumonia. Her sister Hannah went to the Augustana dormitory to be with her until their mother could come and care for her. Both girls finally recovered.

With the cold weather, it was hard for Berger and Lela to keep their apartment and barber shop warm, especially the barber shop where the door was continuously being opened and closed. The cold wind came in with each customer who entered. Berger wore his heavy sweater under his barber's jacket to keep warm. He tried to be careful because he remembered last year when he had the grippe, what a difficult time it was to recover. However, in his work, he was in such close contact with people that the flu bug soon got him. About the middle of January, Berger came down with a cold. It progressively got worse, with a fever and cough. Berger went to bed. The doctor who came to check on him, gave this scary report, *"You have pneumonia."*

Pneumonia was a very serious illness in 1911. There were no medicines to lick it. A person mostly had to try to break the fever and let it run its course.

Within a week, Berger was very ill. Inger came over to help Lela care for him. When Lela realized what the outcome could be, she was very frightened. She couldn't believe that this was happening. Berger was a very sick man. When he went into a coma, Lela knelt by his bed and pleaded, *"Please don't leave me, Berger.*" She buried her head in his quilt and sobbed, "*Please don't leave me.*"

But Berger did not hear her. He never came out of the coma.

The funeral was held at the Methodist Church in Fairview, which was the church they attended, and he was laid to rest in the little cemetery high on a hill about two miles south of Fairview. The bride had lost her groom, Andrew and Inger had lost a son, and Andrew had lost another member of his *Indseth Family Orchestra.*

Everyone was shocked. The town's friend and barber was gone. It happened so fast.

The newspaper wrote...

> "One of the saddest deaths in the county lately is that of Berger Indseth of Fairview, who caught a bad cold ten days ago, which turned into pneumonia, causing death Friday. He was married six weeks ago, had established a good business – he was Fairview's barber – and life held all possible attractions for him. His taking away is sad indeed.
>
> He was the son of Professor Indseth and was a steady industrious man, well liked by all who knew him. Berger Indseth was well known in Canton as this city was at one time his home.

Lela returned to her parent's home in Lennox, but for Lela, Andrew and Inger, the pain of their loss was heart-wrenching. When it became a reality that Berger was really gone, Andrew and Inger would sit and share their feelings with each other.

"It isn't supposed to be this way," Andrew said. "The children are not supposed to go before their parents."

Inger kept repeating what Andrew's mother had written when his father had died... "*Den dag, den sorg. Den dag, den sorg.*" (Each day has its own sorrows.)

There was a question on Andrew's mind, "Many of us were praying for Berger's health, didn't God hear our prayers?"

Inger couldn't answer. She just slowly turned her head from side to side as she contemplated his question.

"I can't believe he's gone," Andrew said as he got up and went to his music room. There he picked up his violin. His violin had always been his comfort. But now he didn't feel like playing it. He tightened the strings and fidgeted with the instrument; then he took a cloth and polished it. "You can't play happy songs when you have pain in your heart," he told himself.

He picked up his violin again. "Perhaps something in a minor key will match the minor chords in my heart." Andrew and his violin emitted some sad sounds, and then he began to play pieces written in a minor key. The melody of *"Oh, Sacred Head Now Wounded"* seemed to fit his feelings. He played it once, and the melody was comforting. This sound was like a musical salve that soothed the raw edges of his grief. The second time he went over it, the words he was so familiar with kept jumping in....

> *"What language shall I borrow,*
> *To thank Thee, dearest friend;"*
> *For this Thy dying sorrow,*
> *Thy pity without end?"*

"I can't understand, Father," he said as he talked to God, " but this I know....You loved Berger, and You love me, and I've decided that that's good enough for me."

But life must go on. Soon the Indseth family were back to their old routines and schedules but Andrew no longer had that energetic bounce to his step, and he was more serious. He kept busy with practices almost every night. In the summer the Fairview band concerts were every Wednesday and Saturday, and there were special concerts about once a month.

Inger was comfortable in her home near Fairview. Each day she would look to the east and see the steep tree-covered hills so reminiscent of Norway on the Iowa side of the river. The Indseth family lived close to town so it was handy for Andrew and Andy to attend all the Fairview Band activities, and with Roy also in the band now, Inger and Florence often followed along.

*   *   *   *   *

Canton was having a building boom. A new Kennedy Opera House was being built, a new gas engine plant, a new Catholic Church, and an addition to the Anderson Furniture Store. Twelve large new residences were finished and being finished.

In 1911, the Chautauqua ran from June twenty-fifth to July third. After ending in the red in 1908, the businessmen from Canton now were backing the Chautauqua. The program this year included The *Anitas*, a ladies' singing orchestra, *The Chicago Glee Club*, which was a very popular male quartet, and a trombone quartet, besides speakers and lecturers.

The Fairview Band was in demand to perform. Hawarden, Iowa, had invited them to play at their July Fourth celebration in 1911, which was held Saturday, July 8. The Fairview Band was a prominent feature in their celebration. With their twenty-four pieces, they entertained on the streets until the noon hour. Then, at the dinner table, Andrew, their leader, suddenly fell ill. A place was provided for him to lie down and Andy cared for his father the remainder of the day.

But the band boys resumed their entertaining in the afternoon and until evening when they gave their concert even though they had no director. The Hawarden newspaper gave this report of the celebration.....

> "There were some negro minstrels, and a couple of acrobats, and the strong man, who gave performances on the streets to keep the crowd amused, and the bands played most of the time too, and we want to say right here that a good many people were surprised at that Fairview band, for those boys can sure play some lively music, and they also present a fine appearance in their natty new uniforms. That band has improved five hundred per cent since any one from this neck of the woods heard them, and they surprised us all, which bears out the old saying that it is a wise man who knows what his neighbors are up to, when he is not watching them. Those band boys were handicapped too, for their leader, Professor Indseth, was taken ill and could not be with them during the day, but they played right along as finely as any city band.

The next morning when Inger got the report of Andrew's attack, she admonished her husband, *"Nei, Andreas*, you just must slow down. That's what I've been trying to tell you. There's a limit to what you should do." But the next day Andrew was better, and he felt he had to keep all his commitments.

*   *   *   *   *

Inger could hear sounds from the music room. Andrew was giving a vocal lesson. First, there were scale exercises, and then she could hear a tenor voice singing songs. If she had been in the room, she could also have watched Andrew as he had this young man do breathing exercises and practice opening his mouth to get each word out loud and clear.

When the young man left, Andrew came into the kitchen. "That fellow has a very fine tenor voice. Could you hear him, Inger? He's a hired man by the name of Joe Odegaard, who works in the Moe area. He is to sing solo parts with the Moe Male Chorus when they have the special music at Nummedal's Moe Church next Sunday. It's a new group. I'd like to go and hear them."

Sunday morning the Indseth's family buggy headed for Moe. When the family entered the sanctuary of the Lands Church at Moe, Andrew, Andy and Roy seated themselves on the north side where the men were sitting, and Inger and Florence settled down with the women. After the sermon and after the offering was collected, the singing Moe men stood to present their selection entitled *"Only One Step"*, in the Norwegian language. The men's voices came out firm and clear as they sang the first verse; then it was time for Joe Odegaard to solo the refrain.

"Bare et skritt!" (*Only One Step!*) His golden tenor voice flowed out into the sanctuary. There are special times when a soloist connects with his audience...and this was one of those times. Every eye was upon him, and every ear was alert to his voice. Now his clear, rich voice sang..... *"Won't you take that step?"* As he asked the question in song with his beautiful tenor voice, and he came to the last note, the note seemed to hang in the air, as if it was waiting for an answer. The congregation was hushed. It was a few moments before people dared to break the spell and breath deeply again.

During a lifetime, there are only a few musical moments that make such an impression on a person that it is always remembered. To many people in the congregation that morning, the men's chorus and Joe's tenor solo were never forgotten.

Andrew paid close attention to Joe's performance. He was pleased that he sang his part just as they had practiced it. After the service Andrew went to Joe, patted him on the shoulder, and complimented him, "Well done, young man!"

The next project for the Fairview Band was a two day booster trip to the surrounding towns. The year before, a booster group from Omaha, Nebraska, had stopped in Fairview, Canton, and all the towns along the railway line. They had a specially made railroad car that they traveled in and they were advertising Omaha at each stop. The Fairview Band boys thought this was a good idea. They would make a booster trip, advertising Fairview and their band, but they would travel in five automobiles, and would pass through twenty-five towns in Iowa, South Dakota and Minnesota, giving open air concerts at each place.

The band left Fairview early on Monday morning, August 7, and played in Hudson at 7:30 a.m., going to Rock Valley, Inwood and around by Rock Rapids, Iowa, and other towns in the area, to Ellsworth and Luverne, Minnesota, where they played a concert at the Opera House Monday evening. The next morning they left from Sioux Falls by way of Beaver Creek and Hills, Minnesota, stopping in Valley Springs and other South Dakota towns along the way. They planned a concert in Canton for Tuesday evening.

The Fairview Boosters and Band arrived in Canton Tuesday evening a little late, but full of music. They gave an elegant concert, which was much enjoyed by all. This was a fine trip for the boys, and would undoubtedly be a boost for Fairview.

The newspaper editor wrote,

> "Leader Indseth has a fine bunch of musicians and he has taught them from the start. His ability as an instructor is First Class and his Fairview Band proves it. Canton enjoyed the concert, and the honor extended to it."

On August 4, the Fairview Cornet Band gave an ice cream social and band concert, which was a grand success. There was a large crowd from Canton, Inwood, Hudson, and the surrounding country. It was an ideal evening and everybody came out and helped make it an enjoyable event. The band boys felt that people appreciated what they were doing in trying to give the town a good band. There was ice cream, hot coffee and sandwiches served during the evening, and the proceeds totaled thirty-five dollars. They were raising money to pay for their new uniforms, and to pay their director.

Chapter 23

"Today I stopped to see how the new Kennedy Opera House was coming," Andrew informed Inger.

"When do they expect it to be ready?" she asked.

"Right now they are planning an opening about the twentieth of October or the first of November. The painters are working inside now. I could see that they were making some very artistic designs in pleasing colors on the walls around the stage opening. It's going to be a very modern and magnificent building. It even has a large balcony.

"The Grieg Chorus is slated to present one of the first concerts in the new facility. It will be exciting to play in such a fine place.....but first we have the Fairview Band concert to prepare for. That's coming up next week on October twelfth."

As Andrew sat and drank his coffee, he was looking out the window. He was fascinated as he watched Inger's ducks waddle across the yard. A neighbor had given her some duck eggs in the spring. These had hatched and now they were half-grown ducks. You could usually see them walking in a row, taking short steps, as they swayed from one side to another in typical duck fashion. Andrew noticed that they had a rhythm to their walk.

"You know, Inger, I think ducks would be a good subject for a musical composition for a band or an orchestra."

"The last band piece you composed certainly has been used a lot. "*The Sunshine March*" has become very popular with your bands."

Andrew's thoughts were still on the ducks. "I can just envision a number called "*Ducks on Parade*" with sounds of their clumsy march movements interspersed with a cheerful tune. I think I'll go to the piano and see if I can work out the idea I have."

Music was always on Andrew's mind.

A large crowd was present in Fairview on October 12, 1911, for the band concert and basket social. People came from all around the area to hear the band boys. The Fairview Band played several fine selections, and then there were a few solos.

Andy Indseth presented a beautiful solo on the trombone and was loudly encored for a second selection. Martin Overseth played a cornet solo, and Mereith Manning and Oscar Tunell presented a piano duet.   E v e r y o n e said that they enjoyed the fine musical entertainment. Following the concert a man from Canton, Lee Stevenson, gave a short exhibition of ventriloquism with his two dolls, Sambo and Jerry.

The next week the Fairview Band boys went to Hawarden to play for Sports' Day. The Fairview Band was getting to be in great demand.

Meanwhile getting a band restarted in Canton wasn't progressing well. There had been three notices in the newspaper recruiting musicians. After the Fairview Boosters gave their fine concert in Canton, and the Canton people saw what wonders Professor Indseth had accomplished in just two years with the Fairview group, they decided that Andrew was who they needed, and they secured him as the leader for the Canton Band again. Andrew had the first rehearsal with that group on Monday evening, October 23, with thirty members in the band. Monday was to be their weekly practice night. Now the idea of a good Canton Band was promising, and everyone expected them to continue to improve.

The Kennedy Opera House was ready. November 24, 1911, was the date for the *Grieg Sangforening's* concert. Everyone was anxious to attend and see the fine new building and listen to outstanding music.

Many automobiles drove up from Fairview with musicians who were taking part in the concert. Andy, Florence and Professor Indseth received rides, and Inger and Roy came along also.

The Grieg Chorus, always good, covered itself with glory on this occasion. They sang with greater spirit and harmony than at previous concerts in the city, and their reputation as singers was well-known. The Grieg concert was all that most ardent lovers of music could ask for; in fact, those who were competent to judge thought it was equal to anything ever given in the state.

The beautiful Opera House, the splendid scenery, and a fine audience may have helped to make the grand musical combination more brilliant and impressive. The balcony, as well as the seats on the main floor, was filled. In fact, the Opera House was packed.

Andrew had put together an orchestra of seventeen talented musicians, eight from Canton, and nine from Fairview. The audience sat in rapt attention as the violins, cellos, flutes, clarinets, trombones, cornets, and a bass fiddle produced such fine music that the people sitting in the audience could imagine they were in Minneapolis or another large city, listening to a fine symphony. Good judges of music and harmony pronounced it the finest musical combination ever heard in the state. The orchestra's excellence was the result of many hours of practicing together. It had the sound of professionalism, and the mark of Andrew's desire for perfection.

Those composing this orchestra were Mrs. Dr. Gulbrandson, Dr. Wendt, I. J. Jacobson, Joseph Anderson and Asa Forrest from Canton. From Fairview were Martin and Anton Overseth, Lawrence Bakman, Oscar Tunell, Mr. Matison, Andrew Indseth, Jr., Miss Florence Indseth and Norman Thackeray.

It wasn't only the men's chorus and the orchestra that excelled. The program included a clarinet quartet, composed of Oscar Tunell, Oliver Gregerson, A. Bakken and Norman Thackeray, and their number was magnificent. The trombone solo of Andrew Indseth, Jr. was one of the finest musical gems of the concert.

Vocal solos by Stella Sogn, Caroline Hermanson, G. S. Hanson and P. A. Sorum won for each soloist the hearty applause of the audience. They were all singers of note, but they sang better and sweeter than usual.

All in all, it was the grandest concert ever heard in Canton, and the Grieg Chorus, as usual, won highest praise, while Professor Indseth and his orchestra delighted everyone. It was a night to remember.

The editor of the *Canton Farmer's Leader* wrote.....

> "Professor Indseth is a born musician, a composer of note, and a leader who has won high honors...
>
> *The Leader* congratulates the Canton Band in securing him as instructor for next summer."

* * * * *

Andrew was at his piano arranging the new piece he had composed for the orchestra. Inger had been listening as he played through it. She rushed into his room.

"*Andreas*, you did it! I could hear the sound of marching ducks. The audiences will enjoy this number!"

"Did you notice how I changed the mood from the merry melody to every now and then returning to the duck's slow clumsy gait?" Andrew asked. He went on, "I plan to get an arrangement ready for the new orchestra's next practice. I am anxious to hear what it will sound like when it is played with instruments."

Andrew slid around to the other side of the piano bench, and invited Inger to sit by him.

"Inger, there is something I need to talk to you about."

Inger sat beside him.

Andrew began to explain the situation that was on his mind.

"Yesterday Andy was sharing with me that he'd like to move to Sioux Falls. It has been hard for him to find a good job here in Fairview, or even in Canton. I began thinking that this would perhaps be a wise move for all of us."

Andrew turned to Inger and asked, "What do you think about moving to Sioux Falls?" He explained, "The main reason we came to Fairview two years ago was perhaps because Berger was here. Now we don't have a special reason to stay."

"What about your bands and the Grieg Chorus practices?" Inger asked.

"There's the Milwaukee Railroad, you know. It can take me from Sioux Falls to Canton for the new Canton Band practice and the Grieg Chorus practices, or to Fairview for the Fairview Band practices, or to Inwood. It should be no problem."

Inger thought about it for a moment and then she confessed, "I guess I'll miss the country life, though, but whatever you decide will be alright with me."

Andrew had made up his mind. "I really believe having Sioux Falls for our home will be best at this time. We need to think of Andy. I know I can be kept busy with private lessons there, and if I get too busy, perhaps I can change some of my other rehearsals to every other week, instead of every week. When I go up to Sioux Falls next time, I think I'll look into housing, but I believe it would be best if we waited until after Christmas before we move."

Inger was thoughtful as she spoke, "It will probably take me that long to get used to the idea of moving. I know I'll miss my chickens and ducks."

Inger then had a request, "*Andreas*, if we are going to be moving soon, I think we should make a trip out to the cemetery. When we move to Sioux Falls, we will be so far away, it will probably be a long time before I have an opportunity to visit Berger's grave again."

Andrew turned to Inger and looked her straight in the eye and promised, "Yes, we will do that." Her request revealed that her grief hadn't gone away. "I'll plan on it," she said. "We should go before it snows." Then after a moment of silence, she added, "I wonder if the peony bush I planted on his grave this summer will come up in the Spring."

"We'll just have to wait and see," was Andrew's comment.

Chapter 24

*J*n the second week of the new year of 1912, Andrew and his family packed up their belongings in Fairview and headed for Sioux Falls. Their move coincided with a spell of frigid temperatures. Andrew had ordered a load of coal, but it was a lengthy process getting the pot belly stove and cookstove set up, and good fires going in them. Warming up a house that had been sitting empty took some time.

The trips in and out, carrying in furniture and boxes had left everyone chilled. As a result, many of the family developed runny noses and sore throats.

Andrew began fighting a cold. Because there were so many errands to run and things to get settled, he did not take care of his cold. After a week, he was coughing both night and day, and running a fever.

Inger scolded him, "*Andreas*, you stay inside by the stove until you get over this sickness. I insist."

The last week in January, 1912, was time for Andrew's musical organizations to begin their regular rehearsals after the Christmas break and the Indseth's big moving project. The new Canton Band was to have their regular meeting on Monday night, January 29, and the Grieg Chorus would meet the following evening.

"I think you should cancel your practices. You are in no shape to go out, *Andreas*. Getting into the cold weather and making the trip to Canton will only make you worse," Inger advised.

Andrew considered the situation. He now had a tightness in his chest and was running a fever. He was becoming concerned about his health. But he had an idea.

"Inger, I really hate to cancel the practices when we are just getting started with this new band group. If I get a room at the Rudolph Hotel after practice tonight, I can get a good night's rest and then I'll be in Canton for the Grieg practice tomorrow night. This would save me going down tomorrow." Even though Andrew wasn't well, he felt responsible for his commitments.

It wasn't a very peppy man who boarded the train for Canton on the afternoon of Monday, January 29. Andrew tried to be attentive and get something accomplished at the Canton Band rehearsal. Afterwards he headed for the Rudolph Hotel and went to his room. He asked for an extra quilt to pile on his bed to try to stop the bad case of chills which he now had. However, he didn't have a good night. He had many coughing spells.

The next morning the man sleeping in the room next to Andrew's room reported to Colonel McDermott that he heard groans coming from Andrew's room. Colonel McDermott knocked on Andrew's door and found a very sick man. He called Dr. Morrison to come and check him. Dr. Morrison placed his stethoscope to Andrew's chest, and then shook his head. "Professor, you have a severe case of pneumonia."

"I'd like to get back to my home in Sioux Falls," Andrew said.

But the doctor gave orders, "Professor, you should not travel. The best place for you now is the bed you are in. We'll call your family, and you'll be taken care of here at the Rudolph. I'll come and check on you each day."

Everyone was concerned when they heard of Andrew's illness. Andy, Jr. came down from Sioux Falls and stayed with his father. Members of the Grieg stopped by to check on his condition. On Wednesday Inger came down on the train and spent the day with him. He had not improved. Most of the time Inger sat on a chair by his bed. She was there with a drink of water when he wanted it, and with a cool wet cloth to wipe his hot brow. Often she just sat and held his feverish hand. Inger was very worried; she remembered too well what had happened to Berger. It had only been a year since his passing. Andrew was now so sick he didn't care to converse, and dozed off and on, but when he opened his eyes he always saw her sitting there.

When evening came, Andy said to his mother, "You are so tired, Mother. I think you should go back home and get some rest."

"But someone should be here night and day to see that everything is being done for your *Pappa*," Inger responded.

"I'll stay with him," Andy was quick to offer. "Anyway, it would be more fitting for a man to stay at the hotel. And Roy needs you. He's only eleven years old and shouldn't be left home alone in Sioux Falls."

Andy paused and then he added, "Mother, I think I should send telegrams to North Dakota and Omaha and let Inez, Jenny and Ray know how sick *Pappa* is. Perhaps they should come home."

Rev. Nummedal had made a trip into Canton on Thursday. When he heard of Andrew's illness, he stopped at the Rudolph Hotel to see him. Andrew's condition was worsening every day.

"Friend," Rev. Nummedal greeted Andrew, but Andrew responded with a faint moan. "I am so sorry to see you so sick, my friend," the preacher said. "I do not have medicine for you, but I can give you some comfort from God's Word."

Andrew opened his eyes and listened carefully as the preacher read from Psalm seventy-three:

> "Nevertheless I am continually with Thee;
> Thou dost holden me by my right hand."

Rev. Nummedal gently touched Andrew's hand, and added, "*Jesus loves you Andrew. He'll hold your hand.*"

Andrew closed his eyes. The preacher again gently patted Andrew's hand, and then he left.

By Friday, Andrew was very sick. Andy, Jr. had received word that Inez and Jenny were coming that day, and that Ray would arrive at noon the next day.

The hotel was very quiet. Everyone spoke softly, so as to not disturb Andrew, but there was another reason for this quietness. Everyone knew how critical Andrew was, and there was the dreaded awareness that death was lingering in their surroundings.

On Friday night Andrew passed into a coma, and by Saturday forenoon Andrew's family gathered in his room at the hotel. The doctor had alerted them that the end was near. At noon, Ray arrived from Omaha. Now all of Andrew's family were present. Each member stood in silence around his bed, each with his or her own thoughts and feelings of love, and grief.

Inez and Andy had their arms around their mother at this heart-breaking time. At 2:40 p.m. on Saturday afternoon, February 3, 1912, life's baton was lowered. The musical overture which had been Andreas' life had come to an end. Professor Andreas Kristian Indseth's heart had beat its last beat.

*   *   *   *   *   *

Inger was grief-stricken, but everyone was so kind. Now it was time to plan the church service. Because the *Grieg Sangforening* had been such a special part of Andrew's life, the family chose pallbearers from those friends. The Grieg president, Charles Knudson, offered to help in any way they could.

Inger was so relieved. She told him, "Thank you. You men take care of it ....
the music, and the other details for the service. We would appreciate this."

The floral offerings were many and beautiful. There was a wreath created
in the shape of a music lyre. In the center was an enlarged photo of Professor
Andrew Indseth with his violin. This flower arrangement was placed on an
easel above the casket at the funeral. It was a tribute from his Canton Band.

It wasn't only the family who were grieving. The members of the Grieg
were mourning also. It had been twenty years that he had been the leader of
their successful singing society. They felt they had lost their friend. This was
something they hadn't expected. Why, the Professor didn't even reach fifty-
four years of age!

The funeral service was held in the large new Canton Lutheran Church on
Wednesday morning of February 7, 1912, at 10 a.m. The church was filled.
Besides the people from the Canton area, there were many from Inwood,
Iowa; Beaver Creek, Minnesota; Sioux Falls, South Dakota; the Moe commu-
nity, and from all over the Sioux Valley – people who had enjoyed the concerts
he had led, and persons he had taught and directed.

An appropriate prelude by the new pipe organ set the tone for the service.
Rev. Tetlie conducted the funeral in the Norwegian language. The entire audi-
ence joined in singing, "*Oh Hvor Salig det Skal Bleve Naar Gud's Barn Skal
Komme Hjem*" (O how Blissfully Happy it Shall Be When God's Children
Shall Come Home).

Charles O. Knudson, the President of the *Grieg Sangforening*, translated
the service into English.

The twenty-nine men of the *Grieg Sangforening* who were seated behind
the organ in the balcony, then arose. With heavy hearts they sang the song
they had sung at funerals before, when the Professor had led them. The words
of *Den Store Hvide Flok* (Behold the Host Arrayed in White) had a powerful
message performed with the beautiful blending of the men's voices. The song
settled like a benediction on those gathered there.

President Knudson added his own words on behalf of the Grieg. "We want
to express our sympathy to you, Mrs. Indseth, and the children. Thank you for
all the hundreds of hours you lent your husband and father to us during these
past twenty years. He will be sorely missed.

"With our leader and teacher gone, it would be very easy to '*hang our
harps on the willows*' and discontinue our music, but we know that is not what
our Professor Indseth would wish. We must follow his example and continue
to spread music in our surroundings."

Now, looking in the direction of the casket, President Knudson continued, "I know that the Professor cannot hear me today, but I speak for all of the men, women and young people in whom he planted seeds of music. He was an exceptionally gifted musician, truly devoted to his art. He taught us, he entertained us, and he befriended us. He developed a love of music in our hearts, and with his fine musical training he shared his musical knowledge with us and made our lives richer by adding music to our lives."

President Knudson paused for a moment, and then he choked up as he said, *"Thank you, Mr. Music Man!"*

Following the service in Canton, the casket was removed to the depot and taken by train to Fairview where a service was held in the Methodist Church in the afternoon. The pallbearers there were Fairview neighbors and friends of Andrew. Rev. Pittman conducted the services there.

The church choir sang two numbers – *"Jesus, Lover of My Soul"* and *"Rock of Ages"*, and the Fairview Band played an appropriate band march, but it was a moving moment for those assembled when the band boys began *"Nearer My God To Thee"*.

It was very touching as the cornets, trombones, clarinets, and baritones played the solemn hymn, without their leader. The majority of the listeners had difficulty controlling their emotions.

Finally, *Andreas Indseth's* earthly remains were laid to rest beside his son Berger in the cemetery high on a hill south of Fairview. *Blessed be his memory!*

Epilogue

Following Andreas Kristian Indseth's death, his wife, Inger, with their youngest son, Roy, and two daughters, Florence and Josephine, moved to Washburn, North Dakota to be near her oldest daughter, Inez.

Inger lived only four more years. She was born August 23, 1861, and passed away in 1916, at the age of fifty-five. She is buried beside her husband, Andreas, and son, Berger, in the cemetery south of Fairview, South Dakota.

After his father's death, Andrew, Jr., collected the music his father had composed and made arrangements to have it published in Chicago. He placed the music in a suitcase and boarded the train for Chicago. However, when he reached Chicago, Andrew discovered that someone had stolen the suitcase with his father's music. This was a tragic disappointment for the family, and also for us today, because we would have enjoyed listening to it.

But with Andreas' death, the music did not stop. Andreas Kristian and Inger Indseth left a heritage of talented children, grandchildren and great-grandchildren, where the music has been continued.

Son Andrew, Jr. was a fine musician. He made his home in Sioux Falls, South Dakota, and taught music and played in bands and orchestras in Sioux Falls. He played the baritone, sousaphone, viola and bass fiddle, but the trombone was his favorite. He had four sons who also played instruments, and one daughter.

Ray played the piano and clarinet. He was a restless person, moving from place to place. However, for a time he was a clarinetist in the Minneapolis Symphony Orchestra, and for a time he was a member of a symphony orchestra in Florida.

Andrew and Inger's youngest son, Roy, was only twelve years old when his father died, and only sixteen when his mother passed away, so his oldest sister, Inez, took him into her home. He spent the rest of his life in North Dakota. He had a fine voice, sang in the church choir for fifty years, was a soloist, singing at weddings and funerals, and also sang on the radio. He could play any instrument.

Florence made her home in North Dakota. She taught piano until she was into her eighties.

Josie had three daughters and one son, all musical. The girls traveled and sang as a trio. They were very good. Besides singing, one played the piano, one, the violin, and one, the clarinet. The son played the trumpet, taught music in high school, and also directed the Shrine Big Band.

There were other grandsons and great grandsons who have been high school music teachers and band directors and one who has composed a number of musical pieces. One grandson won trophies for playing the accordion. A number of grandchildren and great grandchildren have fine singing voices; one grandson sings for a living. He has had the lead in musicals; to mention a few, he was the King in *The King and I*, and the fiddler in *Fiddler on the Roof.*

Every Christmas Eve continues to be a musical event in their homes, with musical instruments and lots of singing.

At Christmas, most of the homes have the familiar menu of *lutefisk,* drawn butter, boiled potatoes, *lefse*, and Christmas cookies, and at other times of the year, *sildball* is still a favorite in many of the homes.

The music didn't stop in the organizations Professor Indseth directed either. The Grieg Chorus of Canton, South Dakota, is still in existence to this day. There have been several time breaks with changes of directors, but the group still gives concerts, sings for special events, and they still attend *Sanger-fests*. The *Minnehaha Mandskor* of Sioux Falls, South Dakota also is still going strong. The *Fairview Band* of Fairview, South Dakota, continued into the 1930's.

Martin and Tony Overseth were influenced by the Professor, and music continued to be an important part of their lives. Martin took some musical studies in Chicago, and then moved to Minneapolis where he taught band in a boys' school. He played in the Minnesota National Guard Band, and for many years he was a member of the Minneapolis Symphony Orchestra. Tony spent many months with an orchestra that traveled with "*The Birth of A Nation*", and then he moved to Minneapolis where he filled in at the Symphony when trombonists were needed. Tony was a person like Andrew and Mr. Braein who became emotional over music. After attending a symphony concert, he would be up in the clouds with excitement about special musical moments in the program, still reliving and enjoying them.

Many of the men and women Professor Indseth had inspired and taught continued in their music. Because they had been involved in music and caught a love for music, they passed this interest on to their children. They encouraged them, and so the music really has not stopped but it goes on from one generation to the next.

Now, ninety-four years later, we can say that results of Professor Indseth's musical influence still continues....

and the music goes on!